"Don't frown."

Tony kissed the bridge of h

Kate reared back. "You have to stop this." Instead of determination, her voice carried an appeal.

"Why should I?"

"I don't want to get involved with you," she said, feeling a little desperate.

He raised a hand, curling his fingertips under her chin and tilting her face up to him. "It's too late."

As he forced her eyes to meet his, Kate struggled against an emotional tug. "It isn't too late," she countered firmly, refusing to be affected by a man's mere touch. She was wiser than that. She was stronger. She made a move to step around him. "I know we won't get involved. I won't let us."

He tsked good-naturedly.

She spun back angrily in frustration. "Why aren't you listening?"

His arm at her waist tugged her close, and his mouth captured hers. "You know damn well why."

Dear Reader,

Welcome to Silhouette **Special Edition** ... welcome to romance. Each month, Silhouette **Special Edition** publishes six novels with you in mind—stories of love and life, tales that you can identify with—romance with that little "something special" added in.

This month, Silhouette **Special Edition** has some wonderful stories in store for you, including the finale of the poignant series SONNY'S GIRLS, *Longer Than* ... by Erica Spindler. I hope you enjoy this tender tale! *Annie in the Morning* by Curtiss Ann Matlock is also waiting for you in September. This warm, gentle, emotional story is chock-full of characters that you may well be seeing in future books....

Rounding out September are winning tales by more of your favorite writers: Jo Ann Algermissen, Christine Flynn, Lisa Jackson and Jennifer Mikels! A good time will be had by all!

In each Silhouette **Special Edition** novel, we're dedicated to bringing you the romances that you dream about—the type of stories that delight as well as bring a tear to the eye. And that's what Silhouette **Special Edition** is all about—special books by special authors for special readers!

I hope you enjoy this book and all of the stories to come.

Sincerely,

Tara Gavin
Senior Editor

JENNIFER MIKELS
A Real Charmer

Silhouette Special Edition

Published by Silhouette Books New York

America's Publisher of Contemporary Romance

SILHOUETTE BOOKS
300 East 42nd St., New York, N.Y. 10017

A REAL CHARMER

ISBN: 0-373-09694-1

First Silhouette Books printing September 1991

Printed in the U.S.A.

Books by Jennifer Mikels

Silhouette Special Edition

A Sporting Affair #66
Whirlwind #124
Remember the Daffodils #478
Double Identity #521
Stargazer #574
Freedom's Just Another Word #623
A Real Charmer #694

Silhouette Romance

Lady of the West #462
Maverick #487
Perfect Partners #511
The Bewitching Hour #551

JENNIFER MIKELS

started out an avid fan of historical novels, which eventually led her to contemporary romances, which in turn led her to try her hand at penning her own novels. She quickly found she preferred romance fiction with its happy endings to the technical writing she'd done for a public-relations firm. Between writing and raising two sons, the Phoenix-based author has little time left for hobbies, though she does enjoy cross-country skiing and antique shopping with her husband.

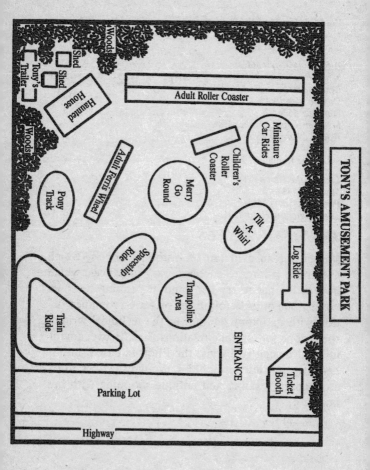

TONY'S AMUSEMENT PARK

Woods
Shed
Tony's Trailer
Shed
Woods
Haunted House
Adult Roller Coaster
Miniature Car Rides
Children's Roller Coaster
Adult Ferris Wheel
Pony Track
Merry Go Round
Tilt -A- Whirl
Spaceship Ride
Log Ride
Train Ride
Trampoline Area
ENTRANCE
Ticket Booth
Parking Lot
Highway

Chapter One

"I've been told that he's a real charmer," Kate Elliot quipped, then moaned softly while kicking up her leg in unison with the other women in the aerobics class.

A tall brunette with ample hips, Joanna Waylon looked confused. Kate knew her co-worker wasn't slow-witted. She just didn't fully comprehend the well-meaning manipulations of Kate's mother.

"Is he the new man in your mother's life?" Joanna managed the question between huffing breaths as the reed-thin instructor rushed them nonstop from leg kicks to knee bends.

"No, you don't understand. Tony Patelli is the new man in my mother's life—for *me*." Kate ignored the piercing pain in her calf. "She caught me at a vulnerable moment two evenings ago—midnight," Kate went on to explain. "I was half-asleep when she called. Barely functional."

Joanna slid a knowing grin at her. "Mothers tend to call at timely moments. So that's when she told you about the charming man she'd met?" At Kate's nod, she commiserated, "Okay, let me guess the rest. She wants to set you up with another blind date."

"No." Kate blew at a strand of hair drooping across her nose. "But I wasn't fooled. She said that he was her neighbor and needed a loan. Would I talk to him? The clinching words sealed the appointment."

Joanna kept smiling.

"'Do this as a favor for me,' Mother said in her sweetest voice." *Soft,* Kate mused. She was definitely too soft where her mother was concerned.

Joanna's perplexed expression returned. "It's early in the morning, Kate. I really don't understand what your problem is."

"The problem is that every time my mother meets an eligible male, she begins planning my wedding. Her latest find owns an amusement park."

Speculation raised Joanna's voice. "Different."

"Even though I haven't met him yet, I would agree. Yesterday morning he came to the bank and filled out the loan application. But he sounds like a dreamer."

"Prejudging, Kate?"

Kate raised her arm, using the pink wristband to blot perspiration on her forehead. As she squatted while Joanna stood, she wondered which one of them wasn't in time with the instructor. "I'm trained to view such people as bad risks." During her banking career, Kate had met others who lacked the perseverance needed to hang on to their investments. "My mother says he's charming... It's not funny," she reprimanded lightly, seeing Joanna's grinning face. "That was my mother's description of him. She's bound and determined to place me on the marriage market."

"Would that be so bad?"

"Yes." Kate squinted against the glare of blazing Arizona sunlight dancing off the window. "I'm thirty years old. I've been married. I'm not looking for another husband."

"Tell her I'll accept her matchmaking."

Mentally Kate grimaced at the quickening tempo of the music, but offered her friend the semblance of a smile. "You only think that you would."

"But you'll see him?"

"Of course." The fact that her mother often failed to exhibit good sense about her choice of companions made Kate less than objective, she knew. "Anthony Patelli—Tony, as my mother calls him, is a friend of hers. What could I do? Say no?"

"I couldn't," Joanna answered.

"I wish I could," Kate murmured. Too many times her mother had lured her into some wacky situation that had left Kate feeling uncomfortable. "Remember last year's costume party to raise funds for wildlife conservation? That time she talked me into being the front end of a horse."

"And this year?"

"This year she's switched her concern from the well-being of furry creatures to the matrimonial status of her daughter." Kate moved more slowly and quickly fell out of sync with the instructor, a willowy redhead who couldn't weigh a hundred pounds. "She's suddenly plagued with fear that I will toddle into my senior years minus a man to lean on, and so she's begun this new campaign of finding her daughter a mate."

Joanna had the good grace to only giggle.

"She's lovingly meddlesome," Kate added, flapping her arms like a chicken and concentrating on the instructor's fancy footwork.

"I don't see why you're fighting her intentions." Joanna drew a long breath. "What are you going through all this agony for?"

"My health."

"Great! You'll reach the ripe old age of ninety-three and who'll care?"

Kate grinned at her, knowing her friend's comment was well meant. But Joanna just didn't understand how much Kate worried about her mother, a lovely woman who just flitted through life. Kate's latest concern for her revolved around where she lived. A fire, ignited by lightning, had started in the woods near her house. Though the blaze had been contained, two days ago another one had forced a camp-fire ban. The smoke engulfing the mountain range couldn't be seen from the city, but Kate worried that the fire might sweep toward her mother's canyon home.

"You seem to have an abundance of charming men in your life right now."

A long second passed before Kate realized her friend had shifted the subject of their conversation to their new supervisor at Westcot Bank, Edgar Svenson. "Don't I?"

"I wanted to get my sister a job at the bank. She worked as a teller in Tucson one summer," Joanna managed to say between breaths.

"So?" Kate responded, still puffing. "That's good."

Joanna nodded instead of answering as she struggled to keep her breathing even. Sighing heavily, she stopped, more inclined to finish the conversation than the exercise. "I thought so until Svenson arrived. Now I don't think I will. He would probably believe that I brought her in and we were conspiring to rob the bank."

Kate pushed back a tendril of blond hair and sent her a doubtful look.

"You never know," Joanna went on. "The man is odd. I've never met anyone so narrow-minded before."

Kate wanted to agree, but in fairness to Svenson, as a loan officer, she herself usually was the same kind of stickler about doing her job by the rules.

Joanna made a half-hearted attempt at the intricate dance step. "Instead of coming to this class, we should have indulged in waffles topped with whipped cream.''

Kate shot a smile at her friend, then caught the time on the gallery clock near the door. At six in the morning, the idea of whipped cream set her stomach somersaulting. By nature she was a systematic person. People ate normal food for breakfast—cereal or eggs—not whipped cream. "It's too early for me."

"You need to learn a little decadent behavior," Joanna teased. "Have you ever missed one of these morning sessions?"

Kate shook her head before drawing a deep breath. "I like schedules. And if I don't do this exercise class before work, I won't fit it in anywhere in my day."

"You need to relax more."

Laughing softly, Kate touched her arm before starting to turn away. "I hear that from my mother all the time."

"Where are you going?" Frowning, Joanna stopped again. "You're not leaving already, are you?"

Kate nodded, backing away. "I have a meeting before the bank opens." Rubbing her calf, she hobbled to the locker room to change out of the leotard and into her clothes.

Joanna really didn't understand her dilemma about her mother. Recently Kate's life had been running smoothly and she wanted to keep it that way. No surprises. No unexpected moments. She didn't want her heart to jump or pitter-patter again over some male, especially one who probably didn't have a serious thought in his brain.

Soot smudged the faces of the men around Tony. His back ached from bending over and digging a trench, a firebreak, through the woods to the road. Beneath the gloves that he wore, his flesh burned. Blisters had broken hours ago, and the canvas of the gloves rubbed against raw flesh with every shovelful of dirt that he moved.

He glanced at his watch, knowing he had to leave soon. He'd been returning from filling out the loan application at the bank yesterday when two pumper trucks had whizzed past on the highway. He'd stuck his head out the window and yelled to the men armed with shovels in the next vehicle, a pickup. A message about another fire had been shouted back at him. He'd followed the men, knowing more volunteers would be needed.

He had a vested interest in those woods that were scorching beneath the blazing sun. If the wind shifted or the fire jumped the road that led to his own property, he'd lose everything.

Hours had passed at a frantic pace. He'd worked alongside the rows of men until after midnight, then had collapsed onto the ground near the fire trucks and had grabbed a fitful sleep. The whirling of a helicopter had awakened him before dawn, and six more hours of the back-breaking task had passed. Three helicopters and two aerial tanks, plus professional fire fighters and volunteers hadn't been able to contain the blaze. The smell of its destruction hung in the air.

Tony glanced up for a moment, eyeing the road that the crew he was part of needed to reach. Hearing the hum of a plane, he threw out another shovelful of dirt before he made himself look up again. Muscles in his shoulders screamed as he stood straight. The noise level was almost deafening—the churning of a bulldozer, the whining of helicopters, the roar of the fire.

The man beside him slowly straightened, too, wiped his brow beneath the yellow hard hat and leaned on his shovel for a second. "Any news?" he asked as the fire boss rushed past them.

"They're bringing in seven crews! The fire is blazing the other way about a mile from homes, but no evacuations have started yet!" the boss yelled over the crackle of the flames.

"Yet," Tony murmured to himself. One of those homes belonged to Claire Elliot Vesterhal. He nudged the shovel again with the sole of his boot and cut into the dry grass.

He wondered what Claire's daughter was like. When he'd asked her while they'd shared a pizza at a favorite restaurant, she'd sent him that mischievous smile of hers. "Katie is a beautiful woman," she'd answered.

Katie, he mused, a sweet nickname for a sweet girl. But then mothers clung to youthful nicknames for their daughters.

Claire had gone on to list more of her daughter's virtues. "She's intelligent. And kind. And—"

He'd laughed then. "When I was in college that kind of buildup about a girl usually meant she had a face *only* a mother would love."

"Well," Claire had responded in her breezy manner, "see for yourself, and if you agree, then—"

"Claire, hold it. I'm going for a loan," Tony had cautioned. "Not a wife."

"I know that. But you might find more than you'd ever hoped for."

Tony doubted that. During a brief phone conversation when he'd made the appointment, he'd heard an all-business, no-nonsense tone in Katherine Elliot's voice.

Within a half hour after arriving at her office, Kate decided that the day wasn't going to go well. While she believed a bank should maintain some caution in its policies on loans, Svenson belonged to the starched-collar Victorian era. Edgar Svenson's round cheeks and jowls shook as he wagged his head firmly. "Foreclose," he said in the pedantic tone that made Kate grit her teeth. "If a loan is delinquent, Ms. Elliot, the bank must take action."

Sensitivity was a curse, Kate decided even as she defended her action, remembering how she'd agonized for the Millers. They weren't deadbeats. They were people down on their luck. "Mr. Miller lost his job and requested time to meet the loan payments."

With a scowl, her supervisor delivered his message loud and clear. She'd been too soft. He pivoted, standing sideways and taking a Hitchcockian pose to scan her office.

Kate knew that he'd find nothing to criticize her about. Unlike some of her co-workers, she'd added nothing personal to her quarters, not even a photograph or small plant. It was a brown room with pale beige walls, drapes and carpet. In the midst of it all stood a brown desk with a brown chair. She preferred the simplicity. At least she'd faced herself honestly once. Because she hadn't had a room of her own until she'd been in her teens, she rarely laid claim to any space now.

Hands clasped behind his back, Svenson stared at the activity in the bank like a general inspecting his troops. "As a loan officer, you must develop a thicker hide," he said in parting.

Kate stared after him for only a moment, then whirled around to return to her desk. Her next appointment was due in five minutes, then she had three more before noon. The first one after twelve o'clock was the *big* favor for her mother, but before that neighbor arrived, she'd somehow have to get a grip on her softness and forget that her mother knew him personally. Shaking her head, Kate doubted that she would ever be callous enough to suit Svenson. She'd been raised by a tenderhearted woman who had the uncanny ability to choose the perfect moment to reach her daughter's soft spot.

* * *

At eleven o'clock, the crew reached the end of the road. Exhaustion seeped from Tony's mind and reached his limbs. They felt mushy, and as he raised a hand to brush grime and sweat from his face, he wondered if even that slight movement might make him collapse.

His thoughts on a shower, he drove back to the amusement park. He was turning into the entrance when his truck began hissing. Time suddenly wasn't his ally.

An hour later, only two minutes to spare before his appointment, he zipped the truck into the bank parking lot. Being a few minutes late wasn't a crime, but from what Claire had told him about her daughter, she was a fanatic about schedules, one of those people who allowed so much time for a shower, for eating— and maybe even for lovemaking.

He doubted that he would make points with her. That leaky radiator hose had consumed the time he'd allotted himself, so instead of arriving showered and decked out in a conservative blue suit, he presented the image of someone applying for a grocery clerk's job. He'd have to hope that she didn't believe only those who dressed for success deserved it.

Mumbling an oath, he pushed open the door and strolled into the bank, wondering why he didn't forget the damn appointment. Nothing pricked a man's pride more than having to ask for financial help or being the recipient of a woman's rejection. But here he was—asking for money and priming himself to hear some woman utter an emphatic no.

He surveyed the half-dozen hallways at the back of the bank. He had a choice. He could play a childish game to choose the correct hallway that led to her office or he could ask someone.

He spotted a blonde standing beside a file cabinet. Cool looking, her fair hair tightly wound in a sleek chignon, she was neat as a pin in a suit as ice blue in color as the sky. Beneath the suit jacket she wore a thin white silk blouse. Crisp and simple, the outfit firmly expressed one message—all business.

Tony knew there were several people he could ask, but he was already only steps from her and had already caught a hint of her fragrance, a light scent.

At the sound of footsteps behind her, Kate spun around. She found herself standing face-to-face with a dark-haired man, a gorgeous one, with the darkest eyes she'd ever seen. Not too tall, he barely edged six feet but was lean and muscular, giving the impression of a man who enjoyed pitting his strength against challenges. At that moment he looked both amused and confused.

"Do they give away road maps in this mausoleum?"

She smiled because he did. "Do you have a problem?"

"It seems so."

Smoothly done, his voice had softened with a subtle innuendo. As an appreciative glint flashed in his eyes that was more flattering than insulting, she decided that he was the kind of man who could tempt a woman. "If you need assistance—"

"I guess I do or I'll be late for an appointment."

Kate eyed his sneakers. He wasn't going to do a great job at impressing that person. She pointed at the information desk. "Marianne can help you then."

"Not you?"

Though she tried not to, she couldn't help smiling again. "Not me."

"Off-limits?" As he took a step with her, his gaze dropped to her ring finger.

Kate released a self-conscious laugh and moved away. "Just not the person you're looking for. Marianne will help you."

"Too bad. Too damn bad."

Feeling a rush of pleasure, Kate sighed inwardly. She'd thought she was immune to a good-looking face and a smooth line. Annoyed, she realized she wasn't.

Tony grinned after her before strolling to the information desk. He listened to Marianne, noting her plastic smile, then followed her directions down a hall and scanned the nameplates on the doors. Spotting the one he was looking for, he ambled forward to the threshold. The office was exactly as he expected. Efficient. No frills. But he didn't have to wonder which office the blonde had disappeared into. Standing in the doorway, he studied her as she sat behind the desk. She looked more like a Kate than a Katie to him. Deliberately he shuffled his feet so she would look up.

He got the smile he'd hoped for. "Still lost?" she asked.

"Nope." The words about an appointment stopped somewhere between his vocal cords and the tip of his tongue, realization hitting him that he had probably already blocked his chances for the loan.

"Look, I'm really busy," Kate said, glancing at the clock on the wall. He stood still, clearly not taking her subtle cue to go about his business. Instead he stared at her with those dark eyes. Disturbing dark eyes, she thought. They made her think of a sultry night—and heat. Too much heat, she mused. She'd felt it before and ignored it, but it sizzled between them again. As he eyed the clock, Kate insisted, "I have an appointment, too. In fact, he's already late."

Grinning, his eyes never leaving hers, he pointed at the nameplate. "No, he isn't."

Kate swore softly under her breath. *He couldn't be.* "Mr. Patelli?"

His grin stretched into a slow smile. "That's me."

Inwardly she groaned. So this was her mother's latest find. His attire was better suited to an outing in the woods than a business meeting. He was dressed in faded, snug jeans that revealed the delineation of muscles and a yellow T-shirt with faded black lettering, which displayed only two words of its original saying—Happiness Is. Anthony Patelli presented a definite picture to her. Usually a person walked into her office best foot forward. His best foot was obviously his left. Unlike his right sneaker, the left had shoelaces and wasn't totally covered with dirt.

"You're Katherine Elliot, right?"

Kate bristled slightly. The question seemed inane. He knew darn well who she was. "Was your act minutes ago—?"

He raised his hands in a gesture of surrender. "I swear. I didn't know who you were."

Kate drew a hard breath. Get a grip on this, she chided herself. *Now.* She was going to ask him to come in, but there was no need. He strolled in as if it were his office and closed the door behind him.

Kate went through the usual formality, anyway. "Have a seat, Mr. Patelli." As he dropped into a chair in front of her desk, a small tightening at the base of her skull emphasized how difficult this appointment might be.

He gave her another of his knock-your-socks-off smiles. "It's funny, but I feel as if I already know you."

"Because of my mother?" she responded, sensing the uselessness of trying to keep the conversation on business only.

"Nice lady."

Kate definitely believed that her mother's good intentions had stretched beyond the good-neighbor policy. Sitting before her was, in her mother's eyes, a handsome E-L-I-G-I-B-L-E male. Wondering just what her mother had told him, Kate mumbled uneasily, "She can be exasperating at times. And I have to wonder, did you really come here for a loan?"

Tony could have offered an assurance, explained that he really needed the loan badly, but it had been a long time since he'd enjoyed even a subtle or mild flirtation. "What did you think I came for?"

Kate shot him a quick, wary look. Taking a long, slow breath, she tempered the storm she felt brewing in her. While she was growing edgier, he continued to grin, lounging in the chair, totally at ease, looking as if he belonged in the office and wanted to sit there all day. She ignored his question and shifted the conversation back to his loan. "About your business, Mr. Patelli—is it operational at present?"

"It needs a few repairs." Tony watched her make a note of the information. Even her handwriting was precise. It reminded him of his second-grade teacher's perfect penmanship.

"You owned another business?"

"A small restaurant."

"It was a fairly successful restaurant," she said, frowning as she skimmed over the details on his application. "Why would you sell it?"

As her brows bunched in puzzlement, Tony searched for an explanation that was honest, but might be acceptable to her. "I needed something that was more..." He paused and moved his hands, searching for the right word. "Well, more—fun." At the slight quirk of her eyebrow he could see that she wasn't impressed by the word he'd settled on.

"But you're the sole owner of the amusement park?"

"Sort of."

"Sort of?" she parroted. Kate didn't need to review his marital status. Her mother wouldn't have sent a married man in her direction, but she had to ask the next question. "What about an ex-wife?"

"No. She..." He paused again. "I'm not married anymore." Tony hunched forward to narrow the distance between them. "Look, to be honest, I wasn't sure if I'd want to keep it, so several people bought shares in it." He set his forearms upon her desk. "There's a list on one of the papers in that file with names of the people who have an interest in it."

"Yes, I noticed. Mostly family."

As she fixed her gaze once more on the loan application, Tony wanted her to look up again, wanted to see her eyes. From Claire he'd learned that her daughter liked buying shoes, collecting salt-and-pepper shakers and watching videos of old musicals over and over again. He doubted that she knew anything about him except what the papers before her contained, but he found himself unexpectedly wanting to know more about her—about this woman who was captivated by the sight of Gene Kelly singing in the rain. Shades of a sentimental woman. A romantic one, he decided, aware that he was feeling a definite stirring of his blood for a woman who'd so far offered little encouragement. "They gave me a dollar each," he added, to encourage her to glance at him.

Almost in unison, she raised her head and one finger. "One dollar?"

Tony couldn't help smiling at her amazed expression. "I understand that's legal and binding. You know, consideration given for—whatever."

Visually she followed the swaying motion of his hand. "Mr. Patelli—"

"Call me Tony," he insisted.

As he grinned, she frowned. "I'm afraid not. The bank would frown—"

Tony drew back and viewed her for a second through a narrow-eyed stare. What was wrong with this picture? he wondered. She'd been friendlier minutes ago outside her office. She couldn't be this serious. No one so young, so beautiful, with such a warm, husky voice could be so serious without effort. "I get the feeling that you're annoyed with me. Why?"

Because you're more than I bargained for, Kate told herself. She had to give her mother credit for choosing drop-dead-gorgeous men. Not one of them had been less than incredibly good-looking. But the one across the desk from her now had an edge over the others. It went beyond looks, Kate realized, but couldn't pinpoint what that extra quality was. She only knew that he accelerated her pulse rate with little effort. "I'm not," she said, hanging on to her firm, polite smile.

"Then why did I meet this really beautiful, friendly woman out there?" he inquired with a gesture of his thumb over his shoulder. "And now I'm getting the freeze treatment?"

Kate had to look away. She had played a game of smiles and words with him before, but hadn't expected to see him again, to have those moments haunt her—ever. She shifted on her chair, lining up her words before answering. "You're in *here* for business, aren't you?" She went on, not waiting for his response. "And I don't mix business and pleasure, *Mr. Patelli.*"

She gathered her thoughts, determined to keep some measure of control over the moment, despite the smile he kept flashing at her. Professionally she'd have to see him again. She couldn't allow mere discomfort to get in the way of her job. "Because I personally took this appointment as a favor for my mother, I'll have to check out the property before I send an appraiser. Would early this evening be convenient?" Kate closed the manila folder to signal the end of the appointment. "I promised to see my mother, and since her home is only minutes from your amusement park, it would be convenient for me then."

"That's fine."

Finally he took his cue and rose to his feet to offer his hand, and Kate forced herself around the desk to accept his handshake. All she wanted now was to finish the appointment quickly. He folded his fingers around her hand and held it for a second—a long second. "I can't guarantee anything," she said, less firmly than she'd intended, watching his gaze shift from her eyes to her lips.

"That's all right." He seemed to pause deliberately, waiting for her stare to meet his. "I'm good at fantasizing."

In a second, with the same speed she'd known in her youth, Kate felt the warmth of color creeping over her face. She slipped her hand free of his firm grip and passed breezily over the real meaning in his words. "You might be," she said, annoyed with herself, "but the bank isn't."

Looking amused, he cocked a brow. "You, either?"

"I'm a realist." Pointedly she stepped closer to the door.

Tony felt her dismissal. It was done smoothly, but he couldn't help feeling as if she'd placed a hand at his back and firmly nudged him toward the door. But despite her cool look, he couldn't get the smoky softness of her voice out of his mind. It lured. Enticed. Made a man wonder if it would sound the same when breathless after lovemaking.

Kate would have sworn that she'd heard him chuckle before he closed the door behind him. She let out a quick breath and whirled around to return to her desk. Annoyed, she yanked open a desk drawer and retrieved a candy from the Tootsie Roll she kept there. Since her thirteenth birthday and a desire for the willowy shape of a *Vogue* model, she'd been trying to break free of an addiction to them. Muttering to herself about the ridiculous weakness that overtook her whenever she was nervous, she unwrapped the candy and was breaking off a small piece when the door squeaked open again. She swung toward the sound.

A grinning Joanna peeked in. "Well?"

"Come on in," Kate said between chews.

Joanna didn't need a second invitation. "Well? What's he like?" she asked without preamble.

"You saw him?"

"He's gorgeous."

Kate kept her eyes down to veil her thoughts. "I bet he was a real hellion at one time," she mumbled. "I felt like a principal, trying to reprimand him for some childish prank."

"And couldn't?"

Kate chewed harder to finish the candy. "He just stared back at me with those dark, smiling eyes, and a certainty that whatever I was saying couldn't be too serious."

"And he annoyed you?"

Definitely, Kate reflected, remembering how something warm and slow moving had skittered through her before he'd closed the door. Perching on the edge of the desk, she reminded herself that she hardly knew the man, but if he'd sprung from the same mold as the others who'd breezed through her life, he would likely play this fantasy out for a little while before going on to his next dream. "He's a fanciful man," she said, defying the feelings he'd stirred.

"Not your type?"

Kate heard the tease in Joanna's voice. "No, not my type. Don't romanticize this, please," she appealed lightly, raising a halting hand.

Joanna stepped toward the door again. "You could turn his application over to another loan officer, couldn't you?"

Kate nodded. "If I was smart, I would."

"But you won't?"

Kate couldn't. She'd striven for an excellent work record and such an action would require explanation. What would she say? She found his smile too appealing? No. First, she needed to admit that his looks were distracting. Once she accepted that, she could bypass the hint of physical attraction and visualize him as a nice, smiling, not too swift, bald-headed man.

As Kate shook her head, Joanna giggled again and reopened the door.

Kate frowned at her friend's odd reaction. "What's so funny?"

Joanna grinned. "I was thinking that you might need to stock up on your supply of candy."

Kate stared at the closed door after Joanna had left for a long moment. How transparent was she? She rounded the desk, grabbing another candy. She wasn't usually so swayed by a man's good looks. In the past she'd sought the more intellectual types. But her mother's neighbor knew how to leave a woman breathless with a simple look. Jerk, she railed at herself. He had a nice smile. He was sexy looking. That was all. It was a known fact that sexy men effortlessly curled a woman's toes.

She moved back behind her desk and plopped onto her chair. For good measure, she consciously flattened her toes inside her pumps.

Chapter Two

It was nearly two o'clock before Kate called her mother. Not taking the time to leave her desk, she disdainfully munched at a sandwich of bologna and cheese on rye while she punched the numbers on the telephone. She usually preferred to eat at a small tearoom in the hotel at the end of the block. It was quiet, classy and dignified, and the coffee didn't taste as if it had brewed for hours. Dropping the unfinished sandwich back onto its wrapper, she reached for the coffee that the delicatessen had delivered. After one sip, a bitterness clung to her tongue.

As the phone stopped ringing and she heard the distinct click, she waited for her mother's hello. Because it sounded drowsy, Kate glanced at the clock.

Her mother loved to sleep until sunset and stay up all night. "Did I wake you?" Kate asked.

"I spent the evening taking photographs of the moon," her mother said over a yawn.

Kate guessed that her mother was in some moon-study stage. Claire planned to open her art gallery next weekend and exhibit some of her photographs, her first show since she'd begun professional photography. So for the past week she'd been anxious, snapping a multitude of photographs in order to have plenty to choose from.

"I needed a night photo to complete the exhibit. You will find time to come to the gallery, won't you?" she asked all in one breath.

Kate heard the note of anxiety in her mother's voice. "I wouldn't miss being there. If you need help before the opening—"

"Oh, that's nice of you. But I thought I'd hire someone. Maybe a young man who could help out in the store and manage the unpacking of the crates that arrive. But I may not have anyone before the gallery opening."

"Be cautious about who you hire," Kate insisted, worried her mother would open her too-generous heart and take the first person in need of a job off the street. "You'll have some valuable artwork on consignment."

"Yes, dear," Claire replied in a tone that forced Kate to acknowledge the role reversal she'd instigated.

She smiled to herself, but wished her mother showed a little more common sense about business matters. For too many years she'd watched her mother struggle, until her second marriage had altered their lifestyle. Kate wanted neither of them ever to experience the same feelings of insecurity again. "I could help on weekends."

"Workaholics need rest."

Pencil in hand, Kate doodled a stick figure onto a sheet of paper and ignored what she believed might be the start of a lecture about matrimony. Swiveling her chair, her gaze fell upon the newspaper. "Is the fire any danger to you?" she asked, her thoughts drifting.

"Oh, no." The airiness of her mother's tone clearly indicated that she hadn't given the idea much consideration. "It's miles away."

Somewhat reassured, Kate relaxed. "I'll probably see you before sunset."

"Wonderful. I've found a quaint little restaurant."

The pencil stilled in Kate's hand. Claire Elliot Vesterhal's propensity for out-of-the-way restaurants had taken them into a bikers' bar one time. "It's not like Satan's Den, is it?"

A laugh colored her mother's response. "You'll never let me live that one down, will you?"

"I'm taking precautions this time."

"No, it isn't like that. It's a nice little restaurant near the gallery. A nice homey place with red-and-white-checkered tablecloths. Mostly families go there."

Kate wrinkled her nose. "I was thinking more in terms of Silver Creek Canyon Restaurant."

Her mother sighed loudly and exaggeratedly. "Too stuffy. And I don't feel like dressing up."

"Okay. We'll go to your latest find, and then I'll stay the night so we can play catch-up."

"I'd like that, Katie."

"Mother—"

"You'll always be my little Katie to me."

Kate couldn't help laughing softly. "I know," she answered as she contorted herself to slide out of her suit jacket while juggling with the telephone receiver. She set the jacket neatly over the back of her chair.

"I'm keeping you, aren't I?"

"No, no," Kate protested, swiveling her chair back and staring down at her latest doodle. Quickly she erased it from the margin of Anthony Patelli's loan application. "I have an application in front of me for a loan. From your neighbor," Kate added meaningfully.

"Oh, you talked to Tony," her mother said with a tinge of interest. "He's such a fascinating man, isn't he?"

Kate didn't hesitate to air her doubt. "That's a matter of opinion."

"Oh, Kate, don't be such a stick-in-the-mud. He's *something,* isn't he? And how many young men his age—what is he?—thirty-three, maybe? How many men that age own a business? I know how important financial security is to you."

"He came in for a loan," Kate reminded her before she could start thinking about her daughter in a state of connubial bliss.

"Oh, approve it, Kate. He's such a nice person."

"Mother, banks don't operate that way. That someone is nice is not a top priority in deciding whether to issue a loan or not."

"So you won't give him one?"

"I'm not sure yet. I have to see the property before I send out an appraiser. My credibility is on the line if his business is in really sad shape."

"You'll stop there first then, and look it over. Of course, that makes sense," Claire said as if that were the most logical solution.

Kate tried to hide her exasperation, aware her mother had shifted into her well-meaning but scheming mode. "Yes, I will, but that's not why I mentioned his loan. I almost made a fool of myself with him."

"You did?"

"I did," Kate admitted, still annoyed with herself. "I questioned his motive for being in my office."

"Oh, dear. How did he respond?"

"Amused."

"Well, he is a charming man."

"Mother, please stop saying that."

"Well, he is."

"Whether he is or not doesn't matter. I thought that you had sent him."

"I did send him."

Kate squeezed her eyes shut tight. "Mother, you have to stop fixing me up with dates. I'm getting paranoid. Please. Promise me no more. Promise me that Anthony Patelli is the last male you send my way."

Her mother was silent for a long second.

A disturbing second, Kate decided.

"That makes sense," Claire finally said.

Opening her eyes, Kate drew back and stared suspiciously at the receiver. Instead of being pleased, she felt uneasy at how effortlessly she'd gained maternal agreement.

"I'm really looking forward to some time with you." Her mother's light tone announced that she wouldn't pay any attention to more serious talk. Kate knew better than to persist. A streak of stubbornness firmly lined her mother's backbone.

"Me, too," Kate answered, unable to resist issuing one final warning. "But this restaurant—"

"It's not unusual." Claire clucked her tongue. "Where is your sense of adventure, darling?"

"I left it in my childhood."

"Well, pretend that you're ten again. Fantasize."

Kate gritted her teeth. If one more person mentioned fantasy to her, she'd scream.

"Promise me that you'll try to be less uptight when you look at his amusement park. It has wonderful potential."

Kate prepared herself for a trip that would be a waste of time.

"And he's so charming," her mother repeated.

"Yes, charming," Kate said agreeably, taking the path that she believed offered the least possibility for more discussion about Mr. Patelli. She'd had her share of charming men with charming smiles, including an ex-husband whose greatest talent was being completely oblivious to serious thought. He was one of the not so rare breed that was great until the going got rough. She gave her head a small shake. The world was full of incredibly good-looking dreamers with irresistible smiles.

Tony returned from his appointment and took a much-needed nap, but lazing around was as difficult for him as twelve-hour workdays were for other people. He spent the early afternoon replacing a gear-shift on the Tilt-a-Whirl ride, then settled on a more restful type of work.

As the sun hovered close to the horizon, he glanced at his watch, not for the first time that afternoon, in expectation of one woman's visit. He couldn't remember any woman having quite the same impact on him during the past year and a half. He felt an unnatural impatience, making him aware of just how much he wanted to see more warmth in Kate Elliot's hauntingly pale eyes.

He'd had a few casual dates with some beautiful women, but he'd never experienced a lasting interest in any of them. Possibly he wouldn't with the cool-looking Kate, either, but she'd clicked something on inside him that he couldn't turn off. Despite her aloof look, she had a warm voice. He wanted to see her again, to understand the subtle contradiction he'd felt.

Responding to the crunch of tires he heard on the gravel driveway behind him, he wheeled away from the merry-go-round he'd been painting. Anticipating the fair-haired Kate, he was nonetheless pleased to see a familiar dark-haired woman.

His sister slid out of her Volvo with less enthusiasm than usual, he noted. A tall, lean brunette with a wild mane of hair, Teresa could have had her choice of any man. The fact that she'd chosen Jon Harmon had never pleased Tony. His brother-in-law was a narcis-sistic bore, but their marriage had at least produced one beautiful child. For Sara, a dark-haired, four-month-old minx, Tony was grateful.

"What are you doing?" Teresa called out. "Put-ting the finishing touches on it?"

"Getting ready for the bank lady." He leaned to one side and balanced the paintbrush on the rim of the can. When he turned back, she was close beside him. As her arms tightened around his neck in an affec-tionate squeeze, he felt tension in the slim body. Hands on her shoulders, he pulled back far enough to see her face and sent her a narrow-eyed, older-brother stare that had always stirred her laugh.

She gave him a half-hearted smile. "You didn't have to go for the loan. You could have dug out the trust fund that Grandma left you and saved yourself all of this agony."

What she said was true, but stubbornly, Tony had vowed to start from scratch and make the park solvent. At the time he'd made the decision, he'd needed to challenge himself. "I can't do that, Teresa. I promised myself—"

She placed a finger to his lips to silence him. "You made that promise when you weren't thinking straight."

He caught the shadow of concern in her voice and pinched her cheek, not too lightly. "Is that right?"

"Yes." She sighed heavily in audible exasperation. "Stubbornness is not a virtue, Tony."

He laughed. "You're great for the ego."

"Anytime." She bent forward and peered at the horse he'd been painting. "What's she like?"

"Who?"

"The bank lady."

Intriguing, was Tony's first thought. Since leaving the bank, he'd wondered more than once what had made Kate Elliot so serious about everything all the time. More importantly, he wondered why that suddenly mattered to him. Then he remembered her scent. It wasn't flowery or sultry, but airy, a light fragrance that made him think of a spring rain. It was a perfume that a less reserved woman would wear, the scent of a sunshiny, smiling woman, one that made him wonder about the woman who'd chosen it. He understood about good old chemistry, and at some point since his appointment with her, he'd decided to stroke the sparks and see what that would ignite.

Loudly Teresa cleared her throat. "Well? What is she like?"

"Tense."

Her dark hair blowing in the breeze, she tossed back her head and laughed. "An odd description."

"An honest one," he returned. When he'd touched Kate's hand, she'd visibly stiffened. His intention hadn't been to make her more uptight. He just hadn't given the act much thought. In his family, greetings included affectionate hugs and laughter.

"Hey?" Teresa inclined her head questioningly. "A new challenge?"

Tony couldn't offer an honest answer. He wasn't yet certain about Kate, but she was playing havoc with his concentration. He breezed past his sister's question and shifted their conversation to her problems. "What's going on with you and Jon?"

"Nothing." She pointed at the largest horse on the ride. "You missed a spot."

Tony peered with her at the white horse with its black mane, black hooves and silver and black saddle. Its head bowed, it reminded him of a porcelain replica of a Dentzel horse that he'd seen on a carousel music box. "Eagle eye," he teased, yanking the cloth that was hanging from a rear pocket of his jeans to wipe paint from his thumb. "Where's my favorite niece?"

"Jon's taking care of Sara."

Tony kept his head down to hide his surprise. His brother-in-law rarely took time from business to play the doting father. "Is the advertising game slow?" he asked, tossing the rag aside.

"No. He's constantly going here and there," she said with a careless wave of her hand.

Despite her lighthearted manner, Tony caught the tinge of unhappiness in her voice. "A lot of business trips?"

"More than I like," she admitted, abandoning her forced smile. "And with Sara—well, she's so young. I can't drag her around constantly from one city to the next and I don't want to leave her with a sitter."

As she avoided his stare, he bent slightly to bring his face in front of her. "I'm here if you need someone to watch her."

"I know you are." She touched his shoulder. "And you or Papa are the only ones I'd trust to take care of her, but I hate to leave her so much. Since Jon was home this week, I asked him to watch her for a while. He needs to spend more time with her." Raising one hand to shield her eyes from the glare of the sun, she turned and checked her wristwatch. "I have to go. If I don't run," she announced, "I'm going to be late for a dinner date." Her face brightened, reminding Tony of his more carefree sister of years ago. She leaned toward him, accepting the arm that he automatically tightened around her waist and quickly pecking his cheek with a kiss. "See you."

"Make sure of that. And bring Sara with," he called after her. He held on to the smile until she drove away, aware that she had never worked up the courage to tell him why she'd really stopped by. Tony had his ideas. Her husband was a dope. He had everything any man could want and was too dumb to realize it.

He surveyed the amusement park with a slow turn of his head, then squatted to cap the paint can. He had a lot of work ahead of him. He didn't mind. He'd been raised by parents who believed idle hands led to no good. Though the work on the amusement park had been therapeutic in the beginning, something to keep him too busy to think, he'd lately begun to view it more with a businessman's eye. If he kept at it steadily, he'd have a successful venture. And then? Then he would need something else to occupy his mind.

He wandered into a nearby shed to clean brushes. When he stopped outside again, heat from the hazy sunlight blasted down upon him. In response to the rhythmic thumping overhead, Tony raised his face. Sunlight glinted off the whirling blades of a helicopter before it disappeared into the mushrooming shroud of smoke lingering nearby.

Feeling sweaty and needing a cold drink, he strolled into the mobile trailer that he'd formerly used as an office, though for months it had served as home, sweet home. He'd lost his real home two years ago.

As if drawn by a magnet, he stared at the framed photograph of his wife and child that was propped on a file cabinet in a far corner of the room. He'd spent months grieving for them, months of wishing for some

way to go on living when he felt dead inside. Now the
dark-haired, smiling woman with the infant in her
arms seemed to be reassuring him that it was time to
do just that, time to put the past behind him.

The next half hour was as rushed as the rest of
Kate's day had been. After her last appointment she
dashed to her car to drive to the amusement park. She
considered herself a fair person, and if she made a
promise, she kept it. But she felt uneasy, even a little
panicky. Why was she letting one man unravel her so?
And the anxiety wouldn't ease, it was as if something
unexpected were about to happen.

While she turned her car onto the gravel parking lot
just inside the entrance of the amusement park, she
flicked on the radio to hear a weather bulletin. Catching the end of a newscast instead, Kate was immediately concerned about her mother.

The blaze had burned through grass and brush and
ravaged dozens of acres of forest so far. Kate knew
that no natural barrier of sand or water stood between the fire and the exclusive mountain homes, including her mother's, that were backed by acres of
pines. Hearing no indication of an evacuation plan,
she switched off the radio again and parked her car
close to the entrance, eyeing the cleared land occu-
pied by amusement rides.

Spread over several acres, the park was bordered on
three sides by trees. As she strolled away from her car,
she noted that everything was scaled down to a child's

size except for a few rides at the edge of the park and the scalloped, brightly painted merry-go-round in the middle. Beneath the multicolored canopy were magnificent-looking carousel horses on brass poles. An admirer of fine things, Kate briefly studied the giant white horse that stood out like a leader.

In the stillness it occurred to her that finding the park's owner might be no easy task. Heading in the direction of the huge plastic bubble that housed the trampoline, she heard the faint trill of a train and changed direction.

A ray of sunlight peeked from behind a cloud and caught the chrome of the train's first car. A baseball cap on his head and a screwdriver in his hand, Tony squatted beside the track. As she stepped closer, she heard the gravel beneath her heels announce her approach. Despite the look of deep concentration on his face, his head snapped back and his eyes zeroed in on her with the swiftness of a hawk diving for its prey. Sunlight made him squint, but his eyes never strayed from her while she ambled toward him. Against her will, nervousness fluttered in Kate's midsection.

"You work long hours."

"Sometimes." This wasn't going to be easy, Kate decided. He was a disruptive man with that damn, quick-forming smile of his. She couldn't ignore her reactions. She found him unnerving. Too unnerving.

"We sort of got off on the wrong foot, didn't we?"

He moved closer, and Kate deliberately took the safest route to escape his eyes; she found herself staring at his odd-looking sneakers.

He chuckled quickly, a deep husky sound that cloaked her with a warm sensation. "Still am, I guess. Honestly, I did plan to come to the appointment all spiffed up, but—"

In that instant she realized why her mother liked him. He had an easygoing manner and little reluctance to draw a smile at his own expense.

As she looked away to scan the park again, she nearly smiled, Tony mused. She'd almost given in to spontaneity, but every time her mood softened, she withdrew as if afraid. Rushing her wouldn't work. "Guess you want to see the rest of it, huh?" He didn't hesitate. He slipped his fingers about her arm. "Come on. We'll walk around and you can scrutinize."

With his touch, warmth came first to Kate's mind. Then strength. And an unexpected shiver of pleasure.

She was overworked, she decided in self-defense. That was what was really wrong. Her mother was right. She had been working too hard, otherwise he wouldn't be stirring her so effortlessly. She'd learned how to veil her emotions, had trained herself not to overreact, but it just didn't seem so easy this time, with this man.

"A mess, isn't it?"

A touch of humor accented his husky voice, but she knew he was serious. Clutter was everywhere. Parts of disassembled rides were strewn across the patchy field, and near the edge of the woods loomed a dark, castle-like structure. She took a step forward, then stopped, more aware of his hand slipping from her arm than she wanted to be. Wondering what had distracted him, Kate looked back and caught a whiff of smoke. In the distance she saw the billowy gray clouds of the fire in the woods, hanging in the air as if they were a lingering afterthought of the flames.

"Volunteers stopped it from heading south earlier today, but..."

Something in the way he said that simple sentence alerted Kate. "Did you help?"

He nodded, his gaze fixed on the hazy smoke that was graying the sky and the mountains north of them.

Kate frowned, surprised. He'd given a first impression of being a whimsical man, carefree and uncommitted, someone who would avoid facing unpleasant things. One act didn't change her opinion, but she realized that she might just be wrong about him. "What is that?" she asked, gesturing toward the castle.

In what seemed like lazy reluctance, he dragged his eyes from her. "The haunted house."

The idea of a spooky thrill seemed out of place to Kate. She frowned. "Don't you think a haunted house for little ones might be too scary?"

"The haunted house was originally part of this," he answered, but she saw a curious glint flash into his eyes.

Kate could have kicked herself. Her question had revealed more of her compassionate side than she'd intended. Somehow she had to keep the next few moments geared to business. "Are any of the adult rides operational?"

"Yes." Tony motioned toward the Ferris wheel, then the merry-go-round. "Want to try one out?" Things he didn't fully understand fluttered inside. He cared about the loan, but realized that he would risk it for the sake of getting closer to this woman. "There's a perfect white horse for a princess," he said, though he wanted to tell her it was too late to slide the mask back on; he'd already seen more than one hint of the real Kate Elliot.

Kate sighed at the weakness she felt toward him. He'd lull a woman, she realized in that instant. He'd speak softly, flash that smile, touch her, and set her off balance before she knew what had hit her. But she wasn't easily distracted from her job. "No, thanks." Looking down at the layer of dirt coating the toes of her highly polished pumps, she felt disheveled—and annoyed, as if she were a long way from her pristine world with its gleaming tiled floor and neat stacks of paper. "I don't know if you can be helped."

Neither did he, Tony reflected. She was keeping her distance admirably, maintaining her professional standing. In the past he'd have accepted such a response from a woman as the sign of a lack of interest. But he felt a temptation to reach forward and ease the pins from her hair, to see it loose around her delicate face, to bury his fingers in the soft strands. He stared at her lips and felt an uncharacteristic impatience. One taste, he wished, moving closer. One kiss and he would stop fantasizing.

"Do you plan to do all the labor yourself?" Kate asked, eyeing the Ferris wheel. The repair work must have been strenuous and muscle-aching, even a little dangerous. Equally dangerous was the man who'd done that work, she decided, as, swinging back to look at him, she felt the warmth of his breath fluttering across her face.

"Most of it." His hand slipped over her arm again. "You know, we're not in your office now. You could relax."

"But I'm still working," Kate said, needing to remind herself as much as him. She felt unsettled by his steady stare and decided to stop dodging what she considered the real problem between them. "I don't know what my mother told you about me."

Tony sensed her discomfort. She looked so frustrated, so exasperated that he wanted to trace the faint frown line between her brows. He wanted to ease her mind and assure her that he was an "okay kind of guy," even as he was tempted to touch her skin, to kiss her and find out if this attraction was more than imagination. "She raved about you."

Kate groaned. "What am I going to do with her?"

He shrugged as if there were no problem. "Why do anything?"

Kate met his gaze and felt her pulse jump. At that moment she wished her mother's antics were her only problem, but had to admit that he exercised an insidious attraction. She discounted looks. Handsomeness really meant nothing. Her ex could flutter female hearts easily, and he was a louse. Something beyond this man's attractiveness, beyond his charm and easy smiles, kept drawing her to him. A warning flashed into Kate's mind to keep her guard up around him. "How can you ask that?"

"I'm not complaining about her choice." His eyes—dark and warm—flicked to her lips.

"You can't be serious."

Lightly he touched a tendril of her hair. "What would be the harm in humoring her?"

"I've learned it's safer not to."

She took a step back, and he watched the strand slip through his fingers. "Safe is dull."

"Dullness isn't a curse."

He smiled then, slowly and a little amused.

"Thank you for the tour," she said quickly.

"I enjoyed it, Kate."

Kate. He'd said her name with the ease and familiarity of an old friend and in the soft voice of a lover. Keep your feet planted on the ground, she reminded herself, but felt him reaching out to her, not for the first time. She really did need to play it safe, needed to walk away and not look back. Then she could pretend that the heat sweeping through her was due to the unusually warm springtime temperatures or the menacing fire miles away. But she'd never been good at pretending. She faced life realistically—honestly. He was catching her off guard at every turn. Why? she wondered. She wasn't easily swayed by a few charming words. Hadn't she learned her lesson about charmers? And once burned, hadn't she vowed not to let fair words and a handsome face lead her again to heartache?

Was it possible that she didn't know how to protect herself from a man like him? Like mother, like daughter? she wondered, turning to stroll toward her car. She felt unsteady. The thought was ridiculous. Being susceptible to a certain type of man wasn't a hereditary trait. Still, she would play it smart. She would present her views about his loan application and the committee could decide. Ordinarily if it was a small house loan, she would recommend approval. But he was asking for a lot. Too much, she decided, recalling the way she reacted every time he was too close to her.

She was steps from her car when she dared another glance back at him. His eyes weren't on her. They were focused on the flames shooting above the tops of trees miles away. Circling over them, three aerial tankers dropped fire-retardant chemicals to battle the blaze. Smoke engulfed the planes. One look at the depth of concern in his frown, and Kate felt worry rise within her. "She's in danger?" she asked almost in disbelief. When he said nothing, but kept staring, eyes narrowed as if he were trying to see what wasn't visible, Kate ran back and tugged at his arm to get his attention. "Is my mother in danger?"

Tony gave her a glance. Panic. He heard it in her voice. To keep her steady, he clamped a hand over her arm as he spoke. "Come on. Let's check it out."

She ran with him to the heavy-duty pickup truck parked on a dirt hill as if abandoned. Kate didn't allow herself too many thoughts about her mother or the danger. He released her arm and raced toward the driver's side. Kate kept moving, rounding the back of the truck, but when she reached for the passenger-door handle, the whip of the wind whirled around her. Until that moment she hadn't noticed what direction the breeze was coming from or where it was heading.

"Get in the truck!" he called, opening his door.

She heard none of the usual laziness in his voice. His command was impatient.

"If the fire jumped the ravine on the other side of the woods, it's only a matter of time."

She wouldn't panic, she told herself, but couldn't suppress the fear rising inside her, threatening to strangle her. She flung open the truck door and climbed in, not needing to ask him more.

He raced the truck out of the driveway and onto the road, leaving a plume of dust in their wake, and she saw animals skittering across the road, rushing for safety, rushing away from the fire—away from her mother's home.

Chapter Three

Tony said nothing while he drove. Two years ago another fire had left him with an unbearable helplessness. If only he could have done something to save Michelle and Joey, but he'd been too late. He wouldn't be now. Another person he cared about might be in danger. Claire Elliot Vesterhal had offered some of the maternal concern that had been spirited away from him at the age of ten, when his own mother had died. If he could do something this time to protect someone he was attached to, then he would.

Sitting beside him, Kate nervously toyed with the strap of her purse while clutching the door's armrest with a white-knuckled grip. "She should have gotten a condominium in the city," Kate said, to herself rather than him. "I told her the area was more for summer homes. But no, she wanted to stay there all the time." Kate knew she was rambling, but also knew that the sound of her own voice kept her from thinking and from visualizing her mother's glass and wood bilevel home engulfed by flames. "Maybe my mother has left her home already." She swiveled to take a look at him. "Do you think that they've begun evacuation?"

He nodded but couldn't give her a personal assurance about Claire.

"She's a stubborn woman," Kate said unnecessarily, still agonizing as she worried that her mother might refuse to leave her home.

The drive along the woodland road paralleled a cool-looking lake. Usually the setting sun cast a warm golden glow onto the rippling water, but the nearby fire's smoke both mantled the scenery with its curtain and scented the air. As they neared a slight incline, Tony veered the truck off the paved highway.

At the sudden swerve onto a dirt road, Kate clutched again at the armrest. "What are you doing?"

"We can't get through on the main road because of the fire."

She had no time to respond. Ahead of them, a rolling ball of flames suddenly blocked the road.

Slamming one foot onto a pedal, Tony braked, U-turned to backtrack, then made another turn. He cut into the woods and took her on a jostling ride over a logging road full of potholes and ruts. Swerving sharply to the right, he barely missed a tree.

Kate shot a worried look at him. "If we get lost, I won't be able to help her."

"I'll get you there," he promised, zipping the truck onto the paved highway again.

As the road crested the hill, the homes began to appear. Her heart pounding as if it would burst through her chest, Kate knew that she needed to calm down for her mother's sake. She couldn't arrive at the house hysterical, that would only add to her mother's confusion. But as they made the final turn onto her mother's street, all her good intentions abandoned her.

Blinding smoke obliterated the view of the woods. A gray fog hovered like a low-hanging cloud over the homes. People running away from them emerged from the haze like ghostly figures.

Tony brought the vehicle to a skidding stop several houses away from her mother's. "Get out!" he yelled, motioning toward the sheriff's car stationed just feet away. "He won't let any cars go through but emergency vehicles!"

Kate slammed her door in unison with his and ran toward her mother's home on the crest of the next hill. Sirens wailed as more fire trucks raced behind them. People rushed past in both directions. And overhead the heavy pewter smoke blocked out the sun but not the eerie red brilliance of the flames.

Kate pushed through the door first. "Mother!" she screamed repeatedly, running from the living room to the dining room and then to a back bedroom.

Bent over, her mother was tossing clothes from a closet into a suitcase. Half of them were falling onto the carpet beside the bed.

Kate grabbed her arm. "What should I take?"

Claire turned, a stunned look on her face. "Oh, thank God! Katie!" A slim woman with frosted-wheat-colored hair, in normal times she was rarely at a loss for words. "I don't know. Katie, I don't know," she said in a tearful tone.

Claire was dressed in something that resembled a burlap bag with a rope belt. The tunic top hung to just above her knees and covered white leotards. While the outfit appeared to have been whipped up in fifteen minutes, the heavy braided gold chain and gold ear-rings that she was wearing were clearly priceless.

Kate reached past her and yanked serviceable clothes from hangers, then rushed toward the dresser and opened a drawer. Her mother's jewelry box in her hands, she looked up to see Tony standing in the doorway.

"What should I pile in the truck?"

"The paintings in the living room," Kate replied, but her words were drowned by another voice coming over a public-address system.

"Attention, all residents! Evacuate immediately!"

Kate slammed down the suitcase and grabbed her mother's arm to steer her toward the door. She saw

Tony standing in the hallway. He lifted a Monet from the wall, then stacked it beside a Renoir.

Scurrying with Kate down the hallway, her mother rambled still, looking bewildered. "I returned home after a late lunch date. They told me that I had less than ten minutes to pack whatever I want. But I didn't know what I wanted," she murmured, stopping and staring at Kate.

"It's all right, Mother. Come on," Kate urged, moving her toward the foyer. She wondered how anyone could make such a decision. Her mother's home contained priceless pieces of art. Kate's stepfather had provided well. In passing, Kate lifted a Rodin statue from the foyer table, then wheeled around. As if frozen, one hand against the sturdy banister, her mother stared helplessly, her eyes on her late husband's painting.

Another warning came over the loudspeaker.

Kate noted that Tony had moved the suitcase and the paintings to the edge of the street. When Kate lingered in the doorway, he stormed back toward her. "What's going on? Come on!"

Kate applied gentle pressure to her mother's arm to prod her to move. She wouldn't budge.

Behind her she heard Tony swear. Sidestepping Kate, he moved to the other side of Claire. "Do you want the painting of your husband?"

Dumbly Claire stared at Kate for a second, then swung a questioning look at him.

"The painting?" he repeated softly.

She nodded. "Yes. Yes. The painting, please."

As he rushed back to the living room and lifted the painting from its hanger, Kate tightened her hand on her mother's arm. She still didn't move.

"Kate, I can't leave."

"Mother, you can't stay," Kate appealed.

"I can't leave," she insisted almost hysterically.

Tony was at her side again. "Claire, come on."

She sent him a pleading glance. "Tony, I can't just leave everything."

"Mother, I know it's difficult, but you can't stay," Kate persisted.

"Kate's right," Tony said, gripping Claire's arm.

Kate was worried, but as her mother glued her feet to the floor, Tony took full command.

"Claire, I don't want to slug you," he warned, "but if you don't move..."

Wide-eyed, her mother gazed disbelievingly at him. "You wouldn't..."

"No, of course he wouldn't," Kate assured her.

"Like hell I wouldn't." Despite the firmness of his tone, he'd lied. He couldn't imagine using such force on any woman, but did consider tossing her over his shoulder if she persisted in refusing to move.

Suddenly, her sense of humour apparently restored, Claire giggled even as tears welled into her eyes.

All Kate cared about was that her mother had moved toward the door.

Chaos greeted them outside.

"Last call!" someone yelled over a loudspeaker. "Leave your homes *now!*"

People rushed down the middle of the street, their arms burdened with possessions. Plainly disoriented, they had gathered both the valuable and the useless.

Kate kept a hand on her mother's arm. Claire stumbled along beside her as if even walking had suddenly become laborious. Tony had run down the incline with the paintings and the suitcase. Seeing him race back up toward them, Kate realized how grateful she was that he'd been with her during this time. Without him, she wasn't sure that she could have persuaded her mother to leave the house.

"Oh, Kate." Claire spoke almost in a whisper, her eyes no longer dulled by the shock of the situation. "Kate, I have to go back."

"Mother, don't start again. You can't go back."

"Kate, I have to. I forgot something," she said in the familiar iron tone that she'd always used to keep Kate in line as a child.

"What did you forget?" Tony asked as he reached them.

"It's a box in the den buffet."

"Mother, no box is so important," Kate tried to reason in her calmest voice.

"This one is. I have to go back," her mother repeated, yanking her arm free of Kate's grip.

Tony blocked Claire's path. "I'll go."

Instinctively Kate flung out a hand to grab his arm and stop him. She missed her mark.

"Stay here!" Tony called back, dashing up the walkway toward the door.

Neither Kate nor her mother moved an inch. Until now Kate had viewed him as an easygoing, rather mild-mannered man, but the command that had colored his tone seconds ago had allowed for no argument. She suddenly wasn't sure about anything regarding him, except that he was making a difficult moment easier for her and her mother.

"He won't find the box," Claire said worriedly. "I shouldn't have let him go in. I should have—"

Kate snagged her arm before she, too, took off without warning.

"Kate, I should—"

The roar of the fire consumed her words. It deafened as the blaze, fueled by thicker grass, soared up trees and rushed to their tops, capturing them in a fiery blanket. Helicopters circled overhead, spraying foam. Smoke mantled the trees that marked the property line behind the houses.

One of Claire's neighbors stood in his shorts, holding a lawn hose, its impotent spray drizzling water over the roof of his home. Sparks flew like a giant sunburst and hit a neighboring roof.

Someone yelled behind Kate and she looked back. A fireman's arm nearly clipped her nose as he nudged her into motion. He propelled her only a few feet. Still gripping her mother's arm, Kate stood at the front of the truck, but couldn't take her eyes off the door of the house.

Heavy ash rained over them and landed to ignite the brush behind one man's home. The flames licked at the ground and curled like a giant snake toward a huge pine in his backyard. Terror closed Kate's throat, and her eyes only glanced at the pillars of fire. Minutes seemed like hours before Tony bolted out of her mother's house, the box cradled in his arms. For a second Kate watched him dance over the fire hoses that snaked across the road, but she didn't wait. She tugged Claire with her around the truck to the passenger door.

By the time Tony slid behind the steering wheel, they were ready to go. Saying nothing, he set the box upon her mother's lap, then flicked on the ignition. More emergency vehicles passed before he could ease the truck down the hill.

Worried by her mother's glazed eyes, Kate draped an arm around her shoulders in a consoling gesture. Claire continued to stare straight ahead, clinging to the box.

"You can drive us back to my car," Kate said softly to Tony. "I'll take her to my place..." She paused as he braked at the bottom of the hill. "What are you doing?"

"Get out," he instructed them.

"Get out?"

"Go to the evacuation center. It's only a half a block away. They're going to need people to help."

Kate rarely backed away from opposition and didn't plan to now. She couldn't believe that he would do so much for her mother and then leave her without a care. Her sudden anger might be unreasonable, but his actions were reminiscent of the day her father had left without giving her mother or her a second thought.

"Your mother needs some place to calm down." His voice seemed a shade softer as he glanced at Claire. "And it's close."

Silently fuming, Kate climbed down and offered a hand to help her mother. When her feet touched the ground, Kate looked back at him, still firmly gripping the door handle. "And where are you going?"

Stretching across the seat of the truck, he grabbed the door handle and yanked it from her grasp. "Back up the hill to shuttle people out of there." His words were almost drowned by the slamming of the truck door.

As he wheeled the truck around, Kate dared herself to look back. Flames bathed the sky with an orange-red glow. Sparks flew beneath the wind's command in a helter-skelter fashion, some landing upon her mother's roof. Kate saw the smoke and turned back, not wanting to see flames ignite her mother's home.

Bedlam, Kate thought when they ambled over the hill to the school, where an evacuation center had been set up. Several television station trucks and ambulances barricaded the street.

Inside the building's gymnasium, photographers and reporters hustled about, interviewing the people who were sprawled on mats and blankets. Along one wall, behind a long table, women stood pouring coffee and handing out sandwiches and doughnuts. Kate noted that one of the women was Louisa Medford, a good friend of her mother's who lived in a canyon that was still far from the fire.

Finding the closest chairs, Kate settled her mother beside her and squeezed her shoulder. She looked pale, but clinging to the box and cradling it against her breast, she managed to give Kate a token smile. Kate wanted to cry for her, but now wasn't the time. She searched for soothing consoling words, but what did one say when everything a person had gathered in her lifetime was gone within minutes? "Thank goodness, your photographs are at the gallery. And you moved so much of your equipment to the store for its opening," Kate reminded her, grasping at straws for encouragement.

Her mother's pale, watery eyes swung toward her. "Yes. I should be thankful for that."

Kate heard the threat of tears and wrapped her arms around her. "Oh, Mother." She hugged her for a long, silent moment. The sharp edge of the box sitting in her mother's lap cut into Kate's hipbone, but she held on until the quiet sobs had stopped.

"I'm being silly," Claire said with an exaggerated sniff. She dabbed at her wet cheeks. "I have so much to be thankful for. You." Her smile grew into a genuine one as she lowered her gaze to the box and placed a hand lovingly upon it.

Her curiosity piqued, Kate curled her hand over her mother's. "What's in this?"

"Don't you know?" Claire asked, her eyes widening slightly in surprise. "Don't you remember this box?"

Puzzled, Kate stared at it for a long moment. She'd thought her mother had sent Tony in to rescue silver or jewelry. Claire lifted the lid, and Kate stared at the scattered piles of candid photos. She drew a hard breath.

"Treasures," her mother said softly. "Memories." Handing Kate a photo, she smiled. "Remember this?"

Kate felt an unexpected giggle rise into her throat at the glossy shot of herself, lying on her back in a mud puddle.

"You were such a mischievous two-year-old."

"And not too particular about cleanliness."

"Oh, you had so much fun making mud pies that day."

Kate slanted a grin at her. "You, too?"

Her mother laughed softly. "Me, too." Straightening her back, she sat forward slightly on the edge of the chair. "Well, I see Louisa is here. We should help. We certainly came out of that better than most. Thanks to Tony," she added.

Teetering between amusement and amazement, Kate swung at her and saw the gleam of satisfaction in her mother's eyes. She had just lost her home and most of her worldly possessions and here she was, more intent on matchmaking than on resolving her own dilemma!

Claire scanned the sea of faces. "Oh, Edith Foster is with her."

"Who?" Kate asked, standing with her mother.

"Louisa's cook."

Deciding that worrying about others would probably be the best thing for her, Kate passed out blankets, while her mother joined Louisa and roamed the room, offering coffee, doughnuts and sympathy. Kate paused beside one five-year-old girl. Curled up on a mat, she lay in the protective fetal position. Carefully Kate placed a blanket over her since the room was cool. Fatigued after the fears of the past hour, she felt weariness seep into her own body and pushed herself to keep moving. If she stopped, she knew that she would collapse.

Inching her way back to her mother, she stepped around a young man who was pouring coffee into cups. An apology on her lips, she started to smile, but the smile never formed as he shifted, blocking her way, lowering his eyes and letting them sweep over her. The look and the disgusting lip-smacking noise he made stunned her. In a room filled with people burdened by sorrow, no one would expect such a reaction from someone who was there to help. But then he didn't seem like the sort of man to help anyone but himself. Furious, Kate raised her chin a notch, but stifled the choice words on the tip of her tongue as people crowded around the table.

Hearing her mother's voice, Kate remained silent but delivered a withering glare at the man, then whirled away. Quickly she crossed to her mother, forcing herself to stay calm. Perhaps she'd overreacted. She'd been doing that lately, she thought, recalling choice moments with Tony.

Rambling something about Louisa, Claire hooked an arm through Kate's and dragged her forward. "Come with me," she said, maneuvering her to the table that the woman named Louisa was standing by. A robust-looking, loquacious woman with a short punk hairstyle, Louisa thrust a coffee cup into Kate's hand. Behind her stood the gray-haired Edith.

"Louisa has asked me to stay at her place for a while," her mother informed Kate.

Kate started to protest.

"Now, Katie, don't argue. I know that you want me with you, but I have a very good reason for staying with Louisa, besides her delightful company," Claire added, sending Louisa a teasing smile that stirred a hearty laugh. Claire patted her daughter's forearm. "If I'm nearby, I'll know when I can return to my house."

Kate wanted to object, to remind her that little might be salvageable. Instead she held her tongue and nodded.

"We'll take good care of your mother," Louisa piped up.

Kate had her doubts, but any warning she might have felt like expressing was swept away by her mother's next words.

"Have you met Edith?" Claire asked, pivoting Kate toward the smiling woman who'd stood silently behind the other two.

Coming from her mother, the question wasn't odd. Kate had met the mail carrier, pest serviceman and even the forest-service ranger near her mother's home. "No, I haven't."

Louisa wrapped a sturdy arm around her cook's shoulders. "She's been a real help tonight, too."

"I was happy to help, Mrs. Medford. You've been so kind to me and my son." Edith beamed at the young man beside her. "Jimmy is helping, too," she added, clearly rather proud.

He swung around with the grace of a matador waving his cape for the bull's final attack. No more than twenty, Jimmy was an angry-looking man. An annoying one, Kate thought as she recalled his adolescent response when she'd passed him earlier.

His thin lips remained in a grim line while Edith introduced them. "My son is staying with me now."

Though his pock-marked complexion didn't detract from his good looks, he had an antagonistic expression in his eyes. Kate saw them pass over Claire with a cursory glance, then felt them sweep over herself, stripping her again in less than a second. She felt anger rise for the second time.

"I never knew you had a son," Claire went on gaily in the manner of someone who'd just returned from a vacation in the Bahamas.

"He's been busy. And—he hasn't had time to visit. But that's different now. He'll stay with me until he finds a job," Edith resumed. "Mrs. Medford has been real generous."

Kate never doubted Louisa's kindness. But it needed a portion of good sense, as well. *Keep an eye on your silver,* she desperately wanted to say as she saw Jimmy's hard mouth spread into a smug smile. Concentrating on Edith's conversation, Kate inched back a step. Her shoulder collided with something as solid as a wall. Even before she looked around, a hand touched the small of her back in a calming gesture.

"Is Claire all right?" Tony asked close to her ear.

Kate drew a stabilizing breath and nodded in response before facing him. Her earlier annoyance with him forgotten, she barely managed a smile. Sweat glistened on his forehead, and soot smudged one of his cheekbones. He looked bone weary. "Has everyone been evacuated?" she wanted to know.

"Even Claire's obstinate neighbor." He smiled wryly, as if simplifying the situation. "He didn't want to relinquish his hold on the garden hose."

Kate forced herself to ask the next question. "And my mother's house?"

"The firemen managed to contain the blaze to the first thirteen houses on the block."

Kate briefly met her mother's eyes. Her home had been one of the unlucky thirteen.

Claire responded with a shuddery sigh and a glance at her watch. "I suppose there's no point in staying any longer."

She wouldn't shake easily, Kate thought. She'd sounded firm, strong. Yet though her mother had always faced catastrophe with a strength that Kate had often admired, she wasn't fooled. Her mother was hanging on by her fingertips to that will of iron. Kate said nothing and moved with her mother toward the doors.

The box saved from the fire still cradled in one arm, Claire discreetly nudged Kate with her other elbow. "Are you being civil to him?" she whispered.

That the *him* was Tony seemed obvious. Kate sent her a look of disbelief. Cupid was present again! "Why would you question it?"

"Because you dumped water from a vase on the last man I sent your way."

"He had fast hands."

Trailing a few steps behind them, Tony had to smile. He maintained his distance, pausing to retrieve a photograph that fluttered to the floor. "Claire. You dropped this."

She took it from him and gave a tiny shake of her head in the manner of someone trying to banish a thought, but tears welled up in her eyes without warning.

Kate's own heart lurched at the glossy image. Her mother and Martin stood ankle deep in the ocean, the wind whipping at their hair and clothing, their eyes only for each other.

"Didn't Martin look handsome?" Claire murmured.

Kate sidled closer. She'd never thought about the love that her mother and stepfather had shared. Now, in a single photograph, she could see the depth of caring that she'd been blind to for years.

Kate wondered why she'd forgotten the warm memories of good days, happy ones. She wasn't prone to self-pity. In fact she detested it, but during the past three years, her failed marriage had blocked out so many of the good times of the past. Sorry, Martin, she said silently as she remembered the wonderful man who'd been a real father to her. Her throat tightening, she blinked hard against the tears.

She looked vulnerable, fragile, Tony thought. He couldn't guess what memories had called for such a tender, yet sad look on her face. He wanted to link a reassuring hand with hers, but the barely perceptible straightening of her back kept him at a distance.

"My mother's staying with Louisa tonight. Would you drive me back to my car?"

Tony nodded, saying nothing; he knew she was full of emotion. He would make a guess she wasn't pleased that he'd seen her close to tears. "I'll meet you outside."

Kate stared at his broad back, grateful that he'd pretended blindness to her second of weakness. Ambling forward to catch up with her mother, she wished she could have told him how special Martin had been, how much emptiness had entered her mother's life—and her own—with his death. But she'd learned the danger of leaning too much upon any man.

Outside, a warm breeze, carrying the scent of smoke, blasted at her. Kate stared at the sky still thick with a heavy grayness. "Call me in the morning," she suggested to her mother, certain people would soon be allowed to return to their homes.

"I will, dear." Claire's hand squeezed Kate's with a reassurance.

The gesture's message was clear. *Don't worry about me.* That wasn't easy to do, Kate thought.

Tony braced a shoulder against a streetlight and waited for her eyes to meet his. "You don't need to worry about her." He motioned with an arm toward the parking lot at the side of the building. "She's a trooper."

As he fell into step with her, Kate twisted the strap on her shoulder bag in a small show of nerves. She wanted to tell him that that outstanding quality didn't run in the family. Apologies were never easy, she reminded herself. "I'm sorry about earlier." Beneath the darkness that mantled them, she couldn't see his face clearly and braced herself, expecting some measure of anger from him. "I didn't know what you were doing earlier or that you were going back to help," she said quickly. "I just thought—"

"Why would you expect the worst?" he questioned, frowning.

She heard bafflement in his voice. What could she say to him? She'd made a mistake. But since her divorce she'd expected little from any man.

Tony could have pressed his point, but didn't need more of a verbal apology. He'd heard it in her voice. "It's forgotten."

Kate found herself smiling. "If you'll drive me to the amusement park so I can pick up my car—"

"I'll drive you home."

She opened her mouth to argue, but his raised hand kept her silent.

"I'll drive you home, and tomorrow you can get your car," he said firmly. "You must be exhausted."

"I am tired," she admitted.

"Did that hurt?"

"What?"

He dipped his head slightly. Catching her troubled look, he suppressed his own annoyance. "Never mind."

Kate lifted her chin a touch, feeling as if he'd jabbed at it. He had good reason, she realized while she slid into his truck. She'd hurt his feelings more than once this evening.

When he settled behind the steering wheel, she muttered her address, received a nod for an answer and resigned herself to a lack of conversation during the drive home. She really was too tired to work at small talk.

Curling up on the seat, she struggled to keep her eyes open, but finally closed them and yawned, letting the drone of the truck's engine lull her.

She wasn't an easy woman, Tony told himself during the long drive back to the city. Her need for independence rubbed him the wrong way, though not because he believed in a woman being a clinging vine. He'd been raised to reach out to people, to help, to offer whatever could be given, not so much in monetary value but in time and compassion and anything that might ease another person's sorrow. He'd felt the same qualities whenever he'd been with Claire. She was a giving woman, a caring one. While Kate seemed to have an equal capacity for generosity, outwardly she held herself at a distance. She seemed to carry not so much a chip on the shoulder but something like protective armor.

Concentrating on the city traffic, Tony flicked on the radio and listened to the latest newscast about the fire. When he wheeled the car into the parking lot behind an adobe-colored apartment complex, the woman sleeping beside him didn't stir.

Adjacent to the building was a lush-looking golf course. But the building itself was of a simple design. He wasn't surprised. He sensed that she strove to keep her life uncomplicated.

As he switched off the ignition, a hesitancy overwhelmed him. He should wake her, but found himself studying her face and not knowing what he expected to see other than what was obvious. She was a beautiful woman. He'd known his share, yet he'd never loved anyone except Michelle. And he didn't know Kate well enough to even consider love. But chemistry—that he couldn't ignore. He'd felt it from the moment he'd first seen her.

He pushed open the truck door and stepped outside. A hot breeze rushed over him. Though the fire was miles away, he could still smell the smoke. He sniffed hard, suddenly aware that he carried it with him. It had been a day he'd like to forget. And remember, he realized when he opened the passenger door and stared again at Kate.

Bending over her, he reached into her shoulder bag and fished through it for her apartment keys. The hint of her perfume held him for a second. The light fragrance offered a welcome relief from the acrid smoke he'd breathed in all day. She made him think of springtime, of freshness and of a new beginning rather than the dark, devastating finish of the fire. He leaned closer, inhaling deeply, shifting his eyes to her lips— lips that tempted him to taste something he imagined would be sweet and warm.

Swearing at himself, he pulled back, tucking the keys into one hand, then moved quickly to slip one arm under her knees and the other around her back. As he lifted her from the truck, she murmured softly. A slender hand curled around his neck as if it belonged there. She wasn't heavy, but Tony felt his legs weakening as she pressed into him, the heat of her breath caressing the side of his neck, strands of her hair tickling his jaw.

Kate stirred slightly, lifting her head from the pillow of his chest, aware they were at her door. Flickering thoughts flashed through her mind. She knew Tony was carrying her. She knew that she should pull away. She took care of herself; men didn't. All the important ones she'd known in her life had always left her. But for one blessed moment she wanted to let someone else look after her. She brushed her fingertip across the stubble of his beard, unable to nudge herself from the pleasure of the hard sturdy body against hers. Uttering a sigh, she nestled her face into the curve of his neck. She felt too much warmth in the comfortable cushion he offered to rouse herself. Tired. She was so tired.

"It's been a long day," Tony murmured in response to her murmuring, bracing a foot against the door and shoving it open. He waited a second while his eyes adjusted to the darkness before moving forward to the sofa.

He lowered her to it but couldn't pull back. Moonlight slanted through the slit between the closed drapes. In the darkened room her skin appeared to be of alabaster. Eyes closed, she looked vulnerable, even helpless, but he doubted she would take kindly to such a description.

His arms bracketing her shoulders, he wanted to draw closer. He knew that he shouldn't, but stared at her mouth, inviting and soft, parted in sleep. Undeniably soft, he thought again. He wasn't a man who took what hadn't been offered. At the same time, he wasn't a man who didn't go after what he wanted. And he wanted her. Leaning closer, he pressed his lips lightly to hers. The kiss carried no intimacy, no sensuality, but desire rushed him as if it had been rumbling like a volcano waiting to erupt.

Her lashes fluttered for a second, and temptation nudged him to take a deeper kiss. Had she strained forward? Had he heard her soft gasp? Or had he imagined all of it? A familiar children's story always ended the same way. The prince kissed the princess, and they lived happily ever after.

Out of the corner of an eye he spotted an afghan draped over the back of a chair and turned away. He couldn't give himself time to linger. He fanned the knitted blanket and laid it over her legs, then strode toward the door. He'd stolen that kiss. She would give him the next one. And there would be a next time, he promised himself.

Chapter Four

A glaring morning sun lighted Kate's living room. She felt the stifling heat even before she was fully awake. It was a sultry, torrid mantle that bathed her with perspiration, though she'd hardly moved. She stretched, extending her curled legs. Only then did she realize that there was no smooth fabric of a sheet beneath her. She felt the scratchy texture of the sofa's tweed finish, and frowning, threw back the afghan from her calves and eyed her twisted skirt. Only her shoes had been removed.

Sighing, she closed her eyes again and lay still as she recalled the previous evening. She couldn't fault a man for kindness, and Tony had shown more than a strong measure of it. She'd been touched, but also unsettled.

He was intrusive. Confusing. For a woman who was usually decisive, she realized how easily he could become an enormous distraction.

Kate pushed herself away from the soft cushions of the sofa to get dressed, sure she wouldn't think about him for a few hours. On Saturdays she spent a half a day at the bank, usually hunched over paperwork. This afternoon she would drive to her mother's house and help her with salvaging. Keeping busy was the answer, she told herself.

She was one step from the bathroom when she realized she couldn't even drive to the bank. Her car was still at his amusement park.

Minutes after her arrival by cab at the bank and intent on solving her problem, Kate cornered Joanna in the women's rest room. "Could I bother you to drive me someplace after work?"

Dabbing blusher at her cheeks, Joanna gazed at her face, seemingly engrossed, and nodded. "I look like a zombie this morning." She scowled and drenched the brush with more color. "Where's your car?"

"I left it at Tony's—"

Joanna scanned her with a woman-to-woman look.

"I left it at Anthony Patelli's amusement park," Kate corrected.

"Back up a minute. If you left the car there, how did you get home?"

"He drove me."

As if magnetized to Kate, Joanna set the blusher compact upon the stainless steel counter before her and faced Kate squarely.

"I told you what happened to my mother. I was in a hurry to get to her and—"

Joanna waved her hand dismissively. "Yes, you told me *that*. And I'm really sorry to hear about what happened to Claire. But you left out the juicy part of this story."

Laughing quickly, Kate turned toward the mirror and smoothed strands of her hair at her temple. "I didn't forget to tell you anything. Nothing happened," she insisted, wishing it were entirely true.

Joanna prodded harder. "He's the wrong type?"

"Immensely wrong," Kate answered firmly, hoping her own mind heard her response while she fished in her purse for her lipstick.

Joanna faced the mirror once more and applied more blusher. "Then maybe we'll see him and you can introduce me." As Kate met her eyes in the mirror, Joanna shrugged. "Eligible males aren't that easy to come by."

"I thought that you were dating an attorney."

"I am. But he's slow."

Recalling too many moments when Tony had stirred her with a look or a touch, Kate spoke honestly. "This one isn't."

Joanna grinned. "Sounds exciting."

"He's also not the marrying kind." At Joanna's quizzical look, Kate quipped, "How many divorced men are eager to repeat the experience?"

Wrinkling her nose, Joanna nodded. "My Perry Mason seems to have the same problem."

Kate smiled at her. "Couldn't you get him on breach of promise or something?"

Joanna exploded with laughter. "Oh, wouldn't that be rich!" She exchanged a smile with Kate. "While I'm driving you today, you can help me plan."

"Be serious."

"I am," Joanna said, despite the sparkle of amusement in her eyes. "And we'll try to organize some idea for you and the Disney man."

Kate shook her head. "No, we won't do that. If I don't see him again, I'll be happy."

Joanna paused in closing the blusher compact. "He is a charmer, huh?"

"Why do you think that?"

"Because you want to avoid him."

"I didn't say that," Kate protested.

Joanna grinned knowingly. "You didn't have to."

Tony shielded his eyes from the glare of a morning sun that promised a scorching day. Water now merely trickled from the hose in his hand, and he dropped it to the ground in disgust and stared at the pewter clouds of smoke above the treetops. If the fire spread toward his property, he couldn't do a thing to stop it. Even the spraying of water on everything had been a futile gesture, but nonetheless something he'd felt compelled to do. He'd used the reserve water supply on his property to saturate the amusement park rides and the buildings, including his trailer, but the heat of the morning sun parched everything, drying up what had been soaked less than two hours ago. All the same, if luck was with him, the wind wouldn't shift the fire toward his property.

He dragged a hand through his hair and turned toward the trailer to change his shirt. He didn't really believe luck governed his life. If it had, he would never have experienced the worst of life's miseries, losing a loved one. And he'd lost two in one swift blow. That wasn't the way of a lucky man.

But by nature Tony was an optimist and knew it. The terrible ache that had buried itself somewhere inside no longer pained him with every breath he drew. He'd learned to smile and laugh again. At first it had been forced, a way of telling those who were still around him that he was okay, even when he really hadn't been. A state of numbness had attached itself to him like a parasite while he'd gone through Michelle's belongings and packed up the baby clothes.

Painful days. He remembered them too vividly and realized they were still close, but at least he was no longer struggling to make even the smallest decision. That much of his private war was finally over.

He could smell the sweetness of clear air, enjoy the sight of a sunny blue sky, respond to the sultry heat of a woman's passionate fragrance. Still, he hadn't really begun to live again—until several days ago.

The final step had been taken. He'd seen a woman who'd reached inside him. How often had he thought of her during the past day—hour—minute? Uttering a soft, self-deprecating laugh, he realized that she'd snagged his heart so quickly, so easily that he was still a little shell-shocked by the speed of his reaction. Maybe that was the way life healed pain. It came, it lingered, then suddenly it disappeared. Maybe he was one of the lucky ones.

The fan on Kate's credenza stirred the warm air of her office, muffling her mutterings about best-laid plans going astray.

She set down the telephone receiver after listening to an irate man grumble about his loan being refused. Too often she'd had her heart tugged when she had to refuse one, but she relied on facts, not on emotions. In all phases of her life. To do so was a safeguard. She'd learned a valuable lesson from her ex-husband. In fact, ex-spouses tended to be the greatest teachers. Because of Gary, she wasn't a bright-eyed innocent any longer. Everyone had to grow up.

Well, almost everyone. She stared down at the loan application Tony had filled out and skimmed the information—UCLA, savings and checking accounts. Facts sometimes meant nothing. Why he would give up a successful business for a high-risk one was what she wanted to know. The man had to be a blithe spirit.

Like a child, he focused his life on fantasy and fun. A man over thirty should grow up.

Sighing, she knew she had to stop thinking about him. It seemed like ages since she'd allowed thoughts about any particular man to waste her time. Why him? She'd dated since her divorce and had never had this problem. Why did being around him feel different?

She sat straighter on the chair. The "why" wasn't important. What she needed to remember was to keep her relationship with him distant and businesslike.

Staring down again at her desk, she jotted a notation on her calendar to get an appraiser to assess his property, then called an insurance agency. If she presented a solid package to the sour-faced Svenson, Tony might still have a fighting chance for his loan.

Setting the receiver back into its cradle, she glanced at the half-eaten croissant that nestled on a napkin at the edge of her desk, then neatly folded up the remains and dropped them into the pastry bag. Shifting her attention to her mother, she zipped through the cards on her Rolodex for the one with Louisa's phone number.

The soft voice of Edith Foster answered. "Mrs. Medford isn't home."

Kate expected as much. Louisa was a tennis buff. She spent more time on the courts than the pros did. "I'm really trying to reach my mother—Mrs. Vesterhal."

"Oh, she's gone, too. She left several hours ago."

"Did she get an okay to go back to her house?" Kate asked.

"I couldn't say," Edith responded.

Kate took an easier route. "What was she wearing?"

Edith was quiet for such a long moment that Kate was tempted to repeat the question. "It was real different," she answered cautiously, clearly trying to be polite.

Kate smiled. That description could suit most of her mother's outfits. Kate took a stab at her mother's idea of casual cleaning clothes. "Was she wearing a bright pink smock and a pair of turquoise pants that gathered at her ankles?"

"Yes. She was wearing those pants, but the top was orange."

Kate grinned and offered a thank-you and a quick goodbye. Her mother had a philosophy about cleaning. She never wore anything black or dark in color, at least not when she faced a dull job. It was a strange theory, but one that seemed to work for her. If she looked bright and cheerful while tackling the most unpleasant tasks, then she would feel that way.

Kate dialed again quickly, this time her own number. To her amazement, her mother had done something unusual, even logical, and had left a message for her. "I'm off to pick my way through the rubble."

Rubble was exactly what Kate found when she parked her car on the street behind one of Louisa's and saw the remains of her mother's home.

Claire's Oldsmobile was scorched, the windows blown. The surrounding woods had been leveled and the ground blackened. Where lush green grass had grown between her home and the one next door stood dried-out, browned shoots. The neighbor to the left hadn't fared any better.

Kate wound her way around the debris that had once been her mother's house, aware that the crunch of the ashes and brittle wood beneath her sneakers was announcing her approach.

Holding a cast-iron kettle in one hand, her mother faced Kate with a weak but determined smile, hovering motionless in the middle of what had once been her living room. At her feet was a twisted, blackened swab of cloth, a remnant of the drapes that had covered the back window.

Quickly Kate crossed the room to reach her outstretched hand. It trembled slightly. "I'm not going to be able to salvage very much, Katie."

"Have you found anything?"

Claire waved a hand dismissively behind her. "Nothing at that end of the house. But..." She paused to reach into the carton that she'd obviously brought with her and retrieved a blue and green clay monstrosity.

A giggle rose in Kate's throat at the sight of the silly and grotesquely formed vase that she'd made for her mother in a third-grade art class. "Wonderful. Such a magnificent piece of art."

Claire slid an arm around her shoulder. "Nothing like starting over."

"Oh, Mother, what a shame! Did you find anything else?"

Claire drew away and stepped over what resembled the Chippendale chair she'd had in her foyer. "A few kitchen utensils."

As something glittered at Kate from between two charred blocks of wood, she squatted and retrieved a gold chain. Then minutes passed of finding nothing. Sighing in discouragement, she dropped a sneaker with a burnt-out toe and pushed her hand into the crumbling ashes of books. When she plunged her fingers deeper into the pile of ash, they closed over an object that stirred her smile. Pivoting toward her mother and holding out Martin's pipe, she acknowledged that it was the hope of finding the small, priceless treasures of the heart that would keep them working.

Clutching the pipe, her mother suddenly smiled—a real smile.

In the midst of the quiet, an engine rumbled noisily, then rattled to a stop. Kate paused in a knee bend at the sight of Tony's truck.

"Our reinforcements are back."

Kate straightened and swung a look at her mother. "Back?"

"Tony left to haul something for Mr. Hecht."

Emotions churned as Kate followed her mother's gesturing hand toward her neighbor. Confused, she realized that she would truly weaken if Tony was too kind, too nice, too thoughtful.

As he rounded the front of his truck, she felt his eyes passing over her. She knew she looked different with her hair loose and brushing her shoulders. At the warmth in his smile, she wished that she hadn't worn the snug faded jeans or the peach-colored T-shirt. Then, deliberately, he stared at her sneakers, and she saw amusement flash into his eyes. Kate groaned inwardly. Neon-pink shoelaces revealed more about Kate Elliot than all those crisp-looking business suits she wore. Still smiling, he offered a nod of greeting. Nothing more. But now, even more than before, she felt the need to keep her distance. She sensed he was wondering about the woman who'd chosen those pink shoelaces.

Kate watched the breeze tousle his dark hair while he moved a scorched piece of timber, then she turned away to rummage through the ruins that had once been her mother's bedroom. She had to face facts, she realized. He had a sneaky kind of allure. He was a charmer, the kind of man who aroused soft feelings in a woman when she was bound and determined to remain cool and indifferent. Lord knows, Kate had been trying just that. Yet because she'd been failing superbly, she had to admit the existence of chemistry. It was something explainable. Logical. Anything logical could be thought through clearly and handled. She could handle it—him, she reassured herself.

It was foolish thinking, she discovered. During the following two hours, she couldn't ignore the jolt she felt every time he looked at her. Her back aching, Kate unfolded from her crouching position. Staring at nails in desperate need of a manicure, she heard Tony mumble something about dinner.

Kate shook her head.

Amazingly Claire wagged her head, too. "Oh, I'd love to go to dinner. But I promised Louisa that I'd be back and then I want to drive to the gallery."

Kate thought she'd managed the sticky situation, but before she could count to ten, her mother had said a breezy goodbye. Kate didn't consider stopping her. She knew what her mother's marching stride meant. Nothing less than a tank would stop her.

As Claire's car pulled away, Tony set a carton of pots and pans upon the truck bed. "Are you hungry?"

Kate looked at him askance, wondering if he was just too stubborn to accept her no about dinner. She wouldn't be surprised if he persisted. He had an annoying determined streak. As he whipped around with a small ice chest in his hand and her stomach growled, as if responding to the mention of food, she felt her resistance melting and let a smile twitch at the corners of her lips. "You're tempting me." She closed the distance to peer into the ice chest. "I might eat a little," she relented, laughing reluctantly.

She ate a lot. Her legs folded Indian style, she perched on the bed of the truck at the edge of the tailgate and dug in to the fried chicken legs like a trooper. As she munched on a celery stalk, Kate stared at the charred remains that had once been an antique desk. Near them were her mother's favorite chair and the cuckoo clock that Martin had bought her in Switzerland. "She's lost so much," she said sadly, more to herself than him.

Sitting behind her, his back against the wall of the truck bed, Tony reached forward, and with the back of his hand brushed back the tendrils of hair flying across her cheek. "Not everything."

The softness in his voice as much as his caress made her swing her face toward him. "She's lost more than most. She didn't have it easy after my father left. He was a dreamer who left her with nothing."

Tony crumbled a slice of bread and tossed it onto the ground. "What do you mean, he was a dreamer?"

"He was an unsuccessful inventor who dreamed that he might be world famous. A silly man," she added, scooting back to lean against the side of the truck. As she bent her legs, she felt a desperate need to make him understand that she wouldn't be eased into a relationship with a man like that—like him. "I never even knew him. He took off for California and never bothered with us once he'd left." Kate looked away from the shadows slanting across his face and watched a squirrel scurrying to snatch a crumb from the ground.

"Do you remember him at all?"

"Vaguely. He was gone before I was four." She felt the old buried anger, the same anger that had stirred when during her childhood she'd seen a classmate with her parents. Then she'd yearned for the father who'd never existed in her life, who'd never wanted to be part of a family. That longing had eventually faded, but Kate wondered at the quick resurgence of the hurt that had once been such a part of her. "Four was a very important age in my life."

Tony's expression grew thoughtful. "Because he left?"

"Because I learned to give up fantasies. Like Santa Claus."

A frown shadowed his eyes, hinting that he saw through her. "Age four is awfully young to give up believing in Jolly Old Saint Nick."

Kate cocked a brow. "Did you like fairy tales?"

Humor suddenly filled his voice. "I never thought about it. My favorite childhood story was *The Little Engine That Could.*"

"Very telling."

He'd heard her tease, something rare, and responded with a smile. "Is it?"

"Oh, yes," she said, smiling in her turn, feeling relaxed. Oddly, she felt comfortable with him and wasn't sure if that was wise. "You believe anything is possible."

"You don't?"

Kate watched his eyes briefly fall upon her lips and heard an underlying message in his question. She wanted to let it pass, but the steady gaze fixed upon her carried a challenge. "I know that our lives were turned around after my mother met Martin Vesterhal. He was a wonderful man who made my mother's life brighter, who took a thirteen-year-old stepdaughter and gave her everything, as if she'd been his own."

Tony didn't miss the affection in her voice when she talked about her stepfather. The warmth caressed him and like a fire seemed to spread through his veins. As she looked away, sunlight slanted across the top of her hair. Glints of gold appeared in the soft tresses. So many colors. Fitting for a woman with so many moods, he decided, but it was her eyes with their haunting paleness that truly enticed a man.

"I worry about my mother," Kate admitted with a sigh, moving her shoulders slightly. "Since his death, my mother has been dating several men. Though one of them is a quiet, dignified man who owns several computer stores, also vying for her affections is a robust, fast-talking Texan who collects wood and whittles statues for a living. Unfortunately my mother leans toward the bearded type with a Southwestern twang and a fondness for chili."

Tony chuckled. "And you think the other one—"

"Of course the other man is right for her," Kate cut in. "If my mother isn't careful she could lose everything that she has to another dreamer. She could . . ." Kate stopped herself. Her mother had already lost a great deal, but could lose still more to a man who made idiotic wooden statues, a man who seemed to have sprung from the same mold as her first husband. Kate shook her head in exasperation; in the past she'd had little luck in getting her mother to listen to such reasoning.

Tony reached into the ice chest. "So you play watchdog and make sure she's not lured too easily?" At her quick nod, he laughed briefly, as if amused.

Kate looked up to meet his eyes and saw the bright red carnation that he was holding. Her heart rate jumped to double time.

"You're kidding me." He twirled the stem of the flower then reached forward and tucked it behind her ear. "Red suits you."

A slow-moving tingle rippled through her. "I never wear red."

"Afraid the world will guess?"

"Guess what?"

He sensed her protest, but couldn't resist touching the skin that looked as soft as velvet. He considered his options for a moment. Only a moment. He glided a hand over her arm and leaned closer, his lips brushing hers. "Your passionate nature."

"You're insane." Kate released a deep, throaty laugh but felt a nervous flutter in her stomach. She didn't want this. She didn't want him to touch her too much. "Don't," she insisted as his lips again hovered close. Instead of the demand she'd intended making, the protest came out in a whisper.

"Why not?"

The huskiness in his voice tugged at her like a magnet, stronger and more gripping than his caress, urging her to move closer, prodding her to stop resisting. Almost breathless, she scrambled for a reason not to get involved with him, almost desperate to find one, to keep herself from being open and vulnerable again. She hardly knew the man beside her and was certain that they had nothing in common. "I bet you like baseball games, don't you?" she asked, remembering the cap he'd worn.

His brows bunched and he slowly nodded his head.

"Well, I prefer ballet."

"Ah, I get it." Amused, he went along with the point she seemed determined to make. "And I hate it."

"See?" she insisted.

He brushed a thumb across the curve of her jaw. "Really important."

"And I prefer French food," she went on, knowing she was inanely searching for reasons that would support her side of what was becoming a silly conversation.

"That's devastating."

She wrinkled her nose, aware that her arguments had little merit.

"You could be fighting the inevitable, Kate."

Kate didn't want to know what he thought was inevitable. She felt a web of intimacy being woven around them. Beneath the denim of her pants, even her thighs felt warmer, as if his hands were already touching her. She moved quickly, sliding forward, then jumping down from the truck. "You're wrong," she insisted, wagging her head.

Before she finished her words, he was at her side, close again. "Claire is a born romantic." Absently he toyed with a strand of her hair. "Maybe you are, too."

As his eyes locked with hers, Kate's pulse skipped a beat. Excitement, she realized, and was furious with herself. "Romantics belong in the Dark Ages."

Tony wasn't discouraged by the defiant tilt of her chin. He'd been told by friends that he had the tenacity of a bulldog and knew it hadn't entirely been meant as a compliment. "You don't believe in happily ever after, either?"

The conversation was bordering on the ridiculous, yet Kate couldn't pull herself free. "How many people believe in that today?"

His knuckles brushed the underside of her jaw. "I do," he said simply.

Nerves jumped beneath his casual touch, and she warned herself to step back, but wanted to cling to the wave of pleasure he sent sweeping over her with a few casually spoken words. "Then you're the romantic."

"Guilty. Undeniably. And willingly." Tony sensed that she was ready to fly from him. Watching the mixture of expressions crossing her face, he imagined the conflict warring inside her. Despite her verbal protests, her rarely seen smiles kept giving him a different message. It was a message he didn't plan on forgetting.

Kate gave her head a shake. If it killed her, she planned on keeping a clear head around this man. "I'm going to put through your application for the loan," she said, trying to direct their conversation down a different path.

Tony's brain stalled for a moment at the quick shift of topic. He nearly laughed out loud at his own slowness, but she'd thrown him off balance. Maybe that was part of the appeal, he reflected. He'd always enjoyed a challenge. "Change of heart?"

"Gratitude." Kate breezed on, noting that his puzzled expression had altered to one of amusement before he turned away to lift the tailgate of the truck. "All that is necessary is that you take out a larger insurance policy."

His chin dropped to his chest and his head swiveled toward her. For a long moment he stared at her as if she were crazy.

"Because of fire, obviously," Kate went on nervously, when he continued to stare at her, clearly dumbfounded.

Frowning, he swung around and dropped his backside to the truck fender. Moving slowly as if taking time to consider her words, he stretched his legs and crossed them at the ankle before asking, "And what is that going to cost me?"

She sent him a quizzical look, as if he'd babbled unintelligible words at her. Instead of annoyance, she felt a tinge of disappointment. If she wanted something, she would be more of a fighter than he obviously was. "You couldn't have expected there not to be some problems." With the toe of her sneaker she burrowed a hole in the soft dirt. "Now if this is just a whim—"

"Whim?" Though his stance remained casual, his eyes darkened and his brows knitted with the dark, troubled look of a man weighing the idea of strangulation.

Kate's caution level rose. He didn't need to speak. With one look he conveyed that he wasn't a man who would take even a hint of an insult lightly. She wondered if a temper hid beneath his quick-forming smiles.

"I don't pursue anything on a lark." He pushed away from the truck and with a subtle shift of his body closed the space between them. "Not anything," he said, softly but firmly.

He stood still for a long moment, and Kate saw heat in his gaze. Her heart thudding, she shook her head and backed away. "I'm not interested in this." The denial sounded flat, even to her own ears. "I knew you weren't my type, but my mother..." Her voice faded as she met eyes that called her a liar.

"She's a very wise woman."

He wasn't listening, not really. She sensed a man with a streak of stubbornness as strong as her own. She'd met her share of obstinate people in business, but hadn't thought a reasoning tone would put him off. Employing an old method, one she'd abandoned years ago, she wiggled her way out of the moment with humor. Taking a step away, she laughed softly. In truth, she'd thought his statement outrageous. "My mother is delightful. Everyone who meets her, loves her. She's amusing and intelligent and has a wonderful gift of the gab, but wise..." She paused and raised a brow meaningfully.

Tony was no fool. For the moment, for the sake of her smile, he gave her the distance she seemed to need.

"Somewhere," Kate said, sweeping an arm toward the burned-down house, "somewhere in there are the charred remains of a horse costume, a hula skirt and a Charlie Chaplin mustache. My mother loves Halloween."

He gestured with a hand in the way someone does when they're directing a driver who's backing into a tight spot. "Back to the hula skirt. Is that hers?"

Kate could have bitten off her tongue. "Mine."

"I'm fascinated."

"Don't be."

"You ask too much." A smile hovered at the corners of his mouth. "I don't know, have never known, a woman banker who could do the hula."

"Forget you do."

He arched a brow. "Would it foul up the image?"

"Tremendously."

Despite her amused tone, Tony didn't doubt the seriousness of her answer. She was neat, precise, even a little reserved. The public image, he decided, glancing again at the shocking-pink shoelaces.

Kate saw his gaze shift downward. He was a perceptive man, she realized. He didn't take anything at face value. Could he tell from something so inconsequential that she was cautious but not afraid to take chances? Few people knew that about her. They saw the prim woman in the banker's-gray suits and thought her dull. They didn't know the woman who owned a bright orange bikini, who listened to Patsy Cline in the privacy of her home, who'd spent one summer during college working in a casino. How could they know her? That woman had existed years before she'd learned that only caution kept the heart from danger. They couldn't know. He couldn't, she reassured herself, taking a peek at the telltale shoelaces.

"You're not what you seem, are you?"

Kate tensed inwardly. People who got too close had access to the heart, she reminded herself. "I could play this game and ask what gave you the clue, but—"

"Your perfume."

It wasn't the response she'd expected. She felt her legs weakening, threatening to sway her against him. He didn't play fair. Not fair at all. He grinned in that maddeningly slow way of his that seemed to invite a person to step closer. God, but he was too easy to like. Far too easy. And too dangerous, she thought not for the first time as she felt both pleasure and desire stirring.

"You know we'll see more of each other, don't you?"

"Only occasionally." As his gaze idly roamed over her face, she spoke quickly, breathing softly. "About business."

He stepped closer, seeming deaf to her protest, and brushed a finger over the petals of the flower. "You want to be logical about this?"

"Logical?" She slanted a wary look at him while she placed a hand upon his chest to keep some space between them. "What is logical to you?"

He leaned forward and brushed his lips across her cheek. "That we get something out of the way."

Breathing unsteadily now, she saw a look of determination in his eyes. Kate knew that the *something* he'd mentioned would be a kiss.

She wanted to draw back. If they wouldn't see each other again, why tempt fate? But as his mouth hovered temptingly close to hers, and his fingers lightly fanned the curve of her waist, pinpricks of pleasure danced across her flesh. No way could any woman act nonchalant at that moment.

When he pulled her closer, none of the thoughts fluttering around in her head seemed to matter. The hand she'd placed against his chest to separate them went limp.

"Kate." He said her name softly, letting it flow sensuously off his tongue as he raised a hand to her face. Seduction wasn't new to him. For hours, Tony had thought of nothing but her and holding her like this. He'd thought of his need, and now all he could think about was her. As he brushed his lips across her cheek, he smelled a sweet fragrance that urged him to take the kiss he wanted. ''It's possible....'' He paused, staring at the dark centers of her eyes, watching them grow larger while he entwined his fingers in her hair. ''We might find out that we have no need to kiss each other again.''

One long second passed—an eternity, Kate thought, staring at his mouth even as he lowered his head. Then her vision blurred and she told herself that he was right. They did need to kiss, to test the unfamiliar. All her uncertainties would fade. She'd know then that nothing existed between them. Absolutely nothing.

His arms tightened and tugged her against him, and, as his mouth covered hers, she felt a pressure far more gentle than she'd anticipated. The kiss was thorough, skilled, roaming lazily, his lips beckoning hers to part and to invite the seduction of his tongue. And her mind emptied, not allowing her to think of anything but the taste he offered. Closing her eyes, she wanted to tell herself that she was acting foolishly, but sensations rippled like wildfire and bubbled through her veins. She'd known desire's heat before, but had it ever felt quite so consuming? She felt the warmth of sunlight on her back, but it was the heat of his mouth that was melting her.

Head spinning, she tightened her grasp on the soft texture of his shirt, desperately trying to tell herself that there was nothing special about his kiss. It had been far too long since she'd allowed any man to give her more than a peck, and she'd forgotten the urgency a passionate kiss could arouse. She'd forgotten the madness it could sweep her toward, the hunger that it churned up. There was nothing special about his kiss. If any man had kissed her like this—so gently, so lingeringly, so potently, she'd have felt the same things. It wasn't his kiss or his taste that was driving her senseless. But even as she told herself to draw away, she couldn't. *He* controlled the moment. *He* held her pliant and willing against him. *He* whipped need through her and had her clinging to him.

Her mouth responded to his while she ran her hands over the strong planes of his face. As his kiss invaded, persuaded, seduced, she needed every ounce of willpower to stop a sigh that wanted to turn into a soft moan. With his hands framing her face again, she battled to cling to reality and key in everyday sounds—the cooing of a dove, the whirling rumble overhead of a helicopter, the scurrying of animals in the woods. But for one breathtaking moment she was tempted to plunge recklessly toward the mindless fantasy of another deep kiss. Exercising pure willpower, she disentangled herself from his embrace. Stunned, she searched for indignation, but it refused to surface.

"So," he asked a little unevenly, "what do you think?" Tony knew what he thought. He wanted to dive with her into a sea of passion. He wanted her beneath him, wild and wanting in her turn.

"So-so," she responded, taking a long, shaky breath.

He stifled a smile. The soft sound of her sigh stirred a token of triumph within him. With some satisfaction, he knew he wasn't the only one feeling as if he were standing on a rocking boat.

"And that's that," she finally managed, waving her hand airily.

Without another word, she whirled away to rush toward her car. Tony smiled at her quick stride. She walked with an easy, fluid movement, swaying her hips without exaggeration. She looked calm, but wasn't. And neither was he. Beneath his hands he'd felt the softness of silk as he'd threaded his fingers through her hair. He'd felt a warm desire curl within him as her mouth had twisted and responded to his. He'd felt her tongue meeting his challenge and had known that this wouldn't be the last kiss between them. Never the last, he thought firmly, as the whiff of her fragrance lingered hauntingly.

It detonated feelings within him unlike any he'd known in a long time. But then everything about her pleased his senses.

As she peeled away in her car, he was certain that she would avoid him now. He'd taken a step over what she considered not so much proper but safe guidelines. That was what he felt whenever he was with her. She liked her life safe, predictable.

He sensed that she expected him to fade quietly out of her life, now that she'd agreed to help him secure his loan. She was wrong—definitely wrong.

A man didn't walk away from a woman who'd knocked the breath out of him.

Chapter Five

He'd worn down her resistance, charmed her. For a few senseless moments she'd allowed him to melt her shield with his seduction. But those moments had been a mistake in judgment. Driving home, Kate vowed not to make that mistake again.

She whipped through the house and into the bathroom to stand under the shower spigot. She needed to wash away the grime, to cool the heat that had warmed her blood and sent desire for him racing down to her toes. Scary, she decided. The body was weak, even if the mind wasn't.

Stepping from the shower, she stared at the carnation he'd given her, which she'd felt compelled to put into a bud vase. The problem was that despite her pep talks, she wasn't as sure of herself around him as she'd like to be. What was even more unnerving, her resistance to him resembled a thin thread, for an eternity seemed to have passed since she'd pondered over or fretted about any man.

At the ring of the phone, Kate flattened the towel to her chest and raced into the living room, ignoring the trail of water she left dripping behind her. Minutes later she'd finished the call and had set up a time to meet her mother for dinner.

As she padded on bare feet into the bedroom to dress, she wondered what to wear to visit her mother's latest find. A homey restaurant where the whole family worked, Claire had claimed, but Kate knew her mother's tendency to minimize the negative. She'd called a few greasy spoons and chili cafés homey, too.

To Kate's relief, no one at Luigi's wore leather or chains or sported tattoos. Judging by the restaurant's understated stucco exterior, she hadn't expected its interior to offer such an old-world ambience of romantic intimacy and warmth. Paneled walls and greenery provided a soft background for the tables and the secluded booths. On each table, along with sparkling silver, glistening goblets and bright red linen napkins, nestled a fresh red rose between two white carnations. An accordionist strolled around the dimly lighted room, quietly playing songs that recalled another country's vineyards, winding, narrow streets, and courtyards with flower-decked fountains.

Impressed, she eyed the waiter standing rigidly in his perfectly tailored tuxedo. Though she'd worn a gauzy summer dress in black, it was almost too casual for this place, she decided.

"You are waiting for Mrs. Vesterhal?"

Kate turned toward the voice. It came from a man of slight stature with dancing eyes. His hair, a salt-and-pepper cap, frizzed as if the tight curls that had existed long ago had grown tired and relaxed.

"Claire is on the telephone," he said with a familiarity that didn't surprise Kate while he gestured toward the reservation desk.

Kate nodded a thank-you and rushed forward. "Mother?"

"Oh, Katie, I'm glad Luigi found you."

Kate glanced at the man; so he was the restaurant's owner. "Yes. Is something wrong?"

"Nothing to be concerned about, but I won't be able to meet you. Stay and have dinner, though. It's such a—"

Kate cut off her rambling. "Why aren't you coming?"

"Louisa has a problem. Edith—you remember Edith—her son is missing. She's so upset, calling everywhere to find him."

Kate frowned, believing she wasn't getting the whole story. At first, hearing the concern threading her mother's voice, she thought that Claire and her friend were overreacting. Jimmy was not a ten-year-old boy.

"Depression is responsible for part of the problem," her mother went on. "He hasn't been able to get a job. And if his probation officer learns that he's missing...well..."

Kate wasn't at all surprised. Jimmy Foster hadn't looked as if he would win any citizen-of-the-year awards. "I don't think that you—" She stopped abruptly at the sight of Tony stepping through the double doors.

She groaned softly. She wasn't prepared for this. Though still dressed casually, this time in a white shirt opened at the neck, slacks and a sport coat, he looked too neat, too irresistibly appealing. He was still feet from her, but she felt his stare, a feathery-light caress roaming slowly over her. As he wound his way around a couple, the man's arm reached out and halted him. He stopped to exchange words and share a laugh. Kate caught herself smiling, too, even though she didn't know what had been said.

"I suppose if he could find a job..." her mother resumed.

Kate turned her attention back to the phone conversation, alert to the speculative tone in Claire's voice. "Mother, I don't know why he's on probation, but I wouldn't get involved."

"Now, Kate." Her voice took on an admonitory tone. "You can't be so judgmental. People deserve second chances. Even Tony has helped those less fortunate."

"Well, you don't have to be the one to give it to Jimmy Foster."

"Yes, dear."

At that Kate gave up. With Tony in her mother's corner, Claire wouldn't listen. Kate would have to try to hammer some sense into her at some other time.

"I'll call you before the opening of the gallery," Claire said in parting, revealing a hint of anxiety about it.

Kate mumbled a goodbye and turned back to the desk to set the telephone receiver onto its cradle. Her mother wasn't the only one with a bad case of nerves. Kate had to remind herself to relax. To count to five. To take deep breaths.

"This is a surprise," Tony said, standing so close behind her that his breath fanned strands of her hair near her ear.

Maddening, she thought. He had a maddening effect upon her. Kate whipped around with every intention of brushing past him. He was closer than she'd expected. So near that she felt heat coming from him. Warm and potent, it seemed to reach inside her. "My mother planned this?"

"She's innocent. I'm guilty."

Despite his smile, Kate raised her head questioningly.

"This is her hangout lately for Saturday night dinner. I knew that I'd find you here."

Kate stiffened. He wasn't going to be an easy man to deal with, she realized. It galled her, but she made herself smile, still aware of the gray-haired man standing nearby, whom her mother obviously considered a friend. For her sake Kate would avoid a scene. Looking amiably at Luigi, Kate did her proud. "I'm sorry I won't be staying for dinner."

"You're missing out on something great," Tony observed. As her gaze swung back and pinned him, he nearly smiled. Even agitated, she was tempting.

"I'm sure the *food* is wonderful," she said stiffly. She wondered if there was any way to avoid him. He was so persistent, she thought irritably, but if she were to be honest with herself, she couldn't totally blame him. Though she'd muttered discouraging words, when the showdown had come, when his arms had slipped around her, she'd accepted them. When he had pressed his mouth upon hers, she'd kissed him back. She sighed inwardly, wishing she knew how to battle not only him but also her own feelings toward him.

Noting Luigi's frown, Kate rushed her next words, not wanting to insult the restaurateur. She wasn't prone to making scenes, to drawing attention to herself or complaining needlessly in public places. "I'm sure that I'm missing a wonderful dinner here, but..."

Looking slightly amused, he said graciously, "Another time, perhaps."

Kate sent him a pleasant smile. "Yes, I'd like that."

Luigi smiled warmly, almost fondly at Tony. "My son is prejudice."

"Your son?" Gaping, she swiveled her eyes from one man to the other. In a way she found both infuriating and charming, Tony was grinning at her.

Luigi lightly patted Tony's cheek. "And my son has good taste," he teased.

Tony slanted a glance at Kate. "Yes, he does, Pop."

"Luigi Patelli is your father," Kate murmured minutes later before stepping out the door ahead of Tony.

"Why the shock?"

"I don't know. I just—"

He slipped a hand beneath her elbow. "You thought that I was hatched?"

Kate couldn't stop a laugh. "No, but my mother made a big deal about the family closeness of the restaurant's owners."

"We are close." He tightened his grip, and with a subtle shift of his hip, brushed against her and urged her across the street instead of down the sidewalk toward the parking lot.

"What do you think you're doing?"

Though she gave him an indignant look, Tony heard a lightness in her tone. "Going for a walk."

"A walk?"

"Yeah, walk. It's simple." He demonstrated with his hands. "You put one foot in front of the other."

"Tony..." Kate started, then stopped. "What is the point to this?"

"I'd like to spend more time with you."

"And If I don't feel the same way?"

He straightened his back slightly, looking aggrieved. "You're not attracted to me at all?"

Kate didn't buy the phony crushed look. "You're fishing for a compliment," she chided, staring at her feet.

"Something to soothe a bruised ego," he said self-deprecatingly.

As he slipped his hand down her arm to link with her fingers, Kate drew a slow, deep breath. She knew she was a terrible liar and whenever she attempted it, she gave herself away. So she took the easiest path and answered honestly. "I'm attracted to you." She sent him a wry smile. "But what is the point to it?"

"You're too smart to ask that question." As she turned her head and looked away, he saw a hint of her smile. He leaned closer, toying with a strand of her hair, and caught the faint scent of her fragrance. It teased him, made him wonder where she'd dabbed that scent upon her body. It made him want to touch her.

She snapped around to face him. "If you're looking for fun..."

He stopped his play with a curl. Stunned by her words, he almost laughed. Didn't she feel what he did? "Fun?"

"Yes, it's something you believe in, isn't it?"

"Sure. Fun keeps life on an even keel."

He would turn her world topsy-turvy, Kate tried to remind herself. She'd had a slice of what he was offering, but more was needed. Much more. Caring. Thoughtfulness. Trust. "It isn't enough," she said softly.

Tony didn't think so, either, but sensed their minds weren't meeting to find out what was missing. "What are you looking for?"

As his breath fluttered across her face, she willed herself to drum up an explanation that sounded reasonably impossible. "Compatibility."

He arched a brow as if troubled by her words. "Too pat an answer, Kate."

Kate was becoming accustomed to having her quips fall flat with him as he smiled or twisted her words, forcing her to take herself less seriously. But she had seen another side of him, too. Underneath all that good nature was a steely firmness that on occasion had allowed for no opposition. Such a balance between humor and assertiveness pleased her.

Pleased? God, she was weakening. She squeezed her eyes shut for a second and drew a hard breath, stunned by the realization. She was probably weak from hunger; it always made her feel unbalanced. Now it was making her forget how really unsuitable they were for each other. The sooner he admitted that, the sooner he would leave her alone. Only then would some serenity return to her life.

"Don't frown."

As he kissed the bridge of her nose, she reared back. "You have to stop this." But instead of hearing determination, she thought her voice carried an appeal.

"Why should I?"

"I don't want to get involved with you," Kate said, feeling desperate.

He raised a hand, curling his fingertips under her chin and tilting her face up to him. "It's too late."

Kate struggled against the emotional tug. "It isn't too late," she countered firmly, refusing to be affected by a man's mere touch. She was wiser now. Stronger.

"Always so positive," he said in a tone that was clearly meant to soothe.

But she didn't want to be calmed and made a move to step around him. "I know that we won't get involved. I won't let us."

"Tsk, tsk," he said good-naturedly.

Frustrated, she spun back angrily. "Why aren't you listening?"

"Don't you know?" he demanded, tugging her against him.

She wanted to protest, but as his mouth captured hers, a moan slipped out instead. She fought for steady breathing. Heat—she tasted it, felt it. He was used to weaving a spell around a woman, she tried to remember. Other men had tried that, too, but they hadn't unraveled every remnant of control within her. This man was different. This man's kiss detonated something inside her that she couldn't ignore.

Within seconds he lifted his head and stepped back as abruptly as he'd pulled her close. Tony had acquired a certain skill on the streets of New York. During the difficult years, while his family struggled to make the first restaurant a success, he'd met his share of opposition in the tactics of neighborhood gangs. He'd learned when to challenge and when to back off, but those gangs had been easy adversaries in comparison to the constant obstacles one particular wisp of a woman kept placing in his path. "You know damn well why."

Indignant words popped into her mind. Men didn't just take kisses from her. She wanted to tell him that, but he turned and strolled away from her. Kate heard his soft, contented laugh. The sound rippled in the air and proved as irresistible, as enticing as his smile and only a touch less dangerous than his kiss. His laughter drew her to him as if he held some unbreakable thread that he used at his pleasure to tug her closer.

For a long moment Kate stared at his back, then noticed that he was heading toward a small walk-in diner. She drew a long breath. Couldn't he see how wrong they were for each other? How would she convince him? she wondered, hearing her stomach rumble with hunger. She was described by people as calm, composed and ambitious, yet her nerves were strung so tightly that she thought they might snap at any moment. She knew that she rarely looked frazzled, but she caught herself now picking away the polish from her thumbnail.

She whirled around and stared at her car across the street. Why didn't she just leave? The thought passed quickly as the aroma of food enveloped her. Kate looked back and saw Tony stepping out of the diner, cradling a hot dog in each hand.

"Here." He offered her one. "I got you one with everything on it. Is that okay?" he asked. The casual tone cost him. Her taste still lingered on his lips, his blood still felt warm with need. But he sidestepped the rush of desire that was racing through him. He couldn't lose his direction or his wits. He sensed that if he did, she would leave him floundering in her wake.

Kate eyed the hot dog in his palm. Baffling. The man was confounding all her expectations. She'd been waiting for him to deliver some well-practiced, persuasive lines when he returned. "Are there onions on it?" she asked, reaching for the sandwich.

"Onions. The whole works." With a glance, he checked the street with her before sliding a hand under her elbow and urging her across. "Does that mean we agree on something?"

She laughed. "Onions?"

Tony deliberately waited until she had her mouth full. "It counts. Small things matter," he challenged. She arched a skeptical brow at him. "Dammit, Kate!" he exclaimed. "We have to find some meeting ground here."

She nearly smiled at his exasperated look. "You're not being reasonable."

He thought that he'd shown an abundance of both reason and patience. "As much as you are."

"Didn't we have this discussion before?"

His gaze clashed with hers. "Let's have it again."

Kate decided he was even more stubborn than she. She sighed but humored him. "I'm ambitious and goal oriented, something that's considered a curse by some," she told him between bites. "I'm moody, reliable and practical."

He sent her an indulgent look. "So far I find nothing earth-shatteringly detestable about any of that."

Kate swiped her tongue at the mustard she felt on her top lip. "Okay, here's the other side of the coin. You're carefree, annoyingly amiable and..." She paused as her last words stirred his smile. "And not too practical," she added meaningfully. "I'm the only child of a divorced woman who followed the same path. You're the son of...of... How many children are in your family?" she asked, meeting his stare.

"Four children. I'm the oldest son," he told her, mumbling between the last bites of his hot dog. "Two of them are scattered right now, opening new restaurants for Pop." Suddenly he frowned. "You know, I don't see the point you're trying to make."

Neither did she. She only knew that she didn't feel as resistant to being with him as she wanted to be. "Maybe you're right," she admitted grudgingly. "But one fact is important. I don't understand you, and you don't—"

"What don't you understand?" He balled the wrapper in his hands, then slipped her car keys from her fingers before facing her, his eyes darker, looking angrier. "Can't you understand that a man could be knocked senseless by the sight of you?"

"That's lust," she said quickly, aware he could sweep her off her feet. "I don't want lust."

"Love? Do you want love?"

"No," Kate murmured. "I don't want either."

"Ah, come on, Kate." His voice deepened with frustration. "Be reasonable."

"I'm very reasonable," she countered.

"No, you aren't. If you were, you would realize a woman can't go through life dodging both. You either want one or the other."

She released a shuddery breath and started to shake her head.

Tony clamped his hands on the sides of her face, stopping her. "Cut it out. I've kissed you. Don't tell me that you don't want anything with me."

She brushed his hands away. "I don't want anything to do with you."

That hurt. It cut through him so quickly that he had to battle the force of her words. "Why?" he asked as calmly as he could.

Kate saw the hurt in his eyes and regretted it, just as she wished she could take back her words. She didn't want to hurt him, but didn't want to be hurt, either. "Because I don't understand you."

Tony took a step back and sucked in a cooling breath. God, the woman infuriated him as much as she enticed him. Though her looks had initially lured him, he hadn't allowed them to blind him, but as she stared him down now, the pupils darkening, turning almost black, while the blue of her eyes deepened in color, he felt as if he were drowning in pools of blue. Desire wrenched at his gut. For in those same eyes he saw the heat of fire and imagined the passionate nature of the woman beneath the cool look. "What don't you understand?" he finally asked, calmer.

"Everything," she said, weary of her own conflicting thoughts. She glanced toward the gray haze lingering in the sky. "You're not even concerned about your park. If the winds shift, you'll lose everything."

Tony knew she was looking for a way to put distance between them again. He couldn't let her do that, but wondered how to explain without saying too much and revealing his own pain. They were both vulnerable. She was afraid to love and he yearned to try again. "Things happen that you don't expect," he said by way of explanation.

"Yes, they do," she admitted. "But if you think ahead, you can sometimes keep disaster from striking."

As if he had no choice, he touched her hair. The strands slipped through his fingers. While sunlight had accented the lighter shades in her hair, moonlight slanted an enticing silver glow across it. "So you try to foresee the future and plan?"

He made her idea sound farfetched. "Not in the way you say it."

"You're fooling yourself, Kate."

No, she didn't think she was. She'd allowed fate to run her life before—and look what a mess it had been!

"You can't plan everything," he said firmly. "Pop always says that you walk a straight line, but every once in a while you have to turn a corner." He cupped her chin to make her eyes meet his. "Sometimes you won't like what's around that corner. But you turn it anyway."

"Any other words of wisdom from Luigi Patelli?"

Amusing memories came to mind. His voice took on a lighter tone. "He bounced each of us on his knee and told us to make our marriage last."

She pulled a face. "Unusual fairy tale for children."

"Code of the Patelli family."

"But you're divorced. You goofed."

Tony reared back. An icy chill raced up his spine. He recoiled from it, hunching his shoulders, wanting to step back. It was a dumb reaction, but he hadn't been prepared for such bluntness. Then he realized that she didn't know about Michelle. He'd almost begun to wonder if his marital status was what was making Kate keep her distance. Some women had a peculiar attitude toward widowers, believing that involvement with them meant living forever in another woman's shadow. Tony hadn't understood such logic, yet because of Kate's reluctance, he'd begun to wonder if she were one of those women. Now he knew differently. "I'm not divorced," he answered softly, watching the play of shadows across her features in the dim glow of the streetlights. Luminous eyes stared back at him. "I thought Claire had told you. My wife died, Kate."

Her body tensed. Her mother had given her bits and pieces of information about Tony, but had failed to include one of the most important. "I'm sorry." The words sounded so inadequate. At that moment she felt lousy. Incredibly lousy. With gloom around them, his eyes appeared darker, almost fathomless, but even as he sent her an understanding smile, she saw tension and sadness in the grim set of his features and wished the ground would open so she could slither into some hole. "I assumed that you were divorced," she murmured. "And you never said..."

"It makes people uncomfortable."

"I wish you had told me. I feel foolish now—foolish and sad that I threw a difficult memory in your face."

"It's been a while." Tony was amazed at how emotionlessly the words came out, yet still felt a hint of the ache that had stalked and weakened and tormented him.

He was opening an old wound in this woman and was suddenly too close to the edge himself. It had come too quickly for him to block it. He stared up at the dark sky, remembering now, remembering too much. They'd all assured him that his son hadn't been aware of anything but a blissful sleep. But Michelle... She'd smelled the gas. She'd flicked on the light switch. Maybe the memory would always be too painful, he reasoned, but he'd learned that happiness was always possible. Going on had been the most difficult step for him. "The investigator from the fire department told me that a gas-furnace leak had probably made Michelle and the baby drowsy."

A baby. She agonized for him, her throat suddenly dry. *Oh, God, a baby.* The pressure behind her lids grew heavier, and she damned her soft spot, looking away, needing the whip of the warm breeze against her face. She'd felt so many of fate's mighty blows, and one had even promised to snatch the very life from her. But how devastating it would be to hold a child and then have to suffer life's cruelest fate! Sadness for him overwhelmed her. Not fair. Life wasn't fair.

A strange silence seemed to surround him. She saw him look up, his eyes blank, and sensed that he wasn't seeing her. Caught up in a different vision, he stood so still that she was frightened for him as she imagined the black days he must have endured. Numbness weighed her down, nearly overcoming her. Never before had she wanted so badly to wrap her arms around a man and offer comfort. Sensing he was past the time of deep grief, she felt its lingering wave. "Tony." She stepped closer and raised a hand to caress his cheek, wanting to touch him, hold him. She could excuse away the need, could pretend that he'd found the way to her heart with his tragic words. She could pretend a lot of things. But she had to admit that he had once again stirred another emotion within her, had made her want to reach out to him.

At her touch, something slammed hard against Tony's chest. He shook his head in the manner of someone banishing a memory. Silently he muttered a curse. She didn't need to say anything. He didn't want her sympathy.

But she was gentle, so damn gentle. Had he questioned his attraction to her before, he knew that by now all doubt would have vanished. Here, in this slip of a woman with her cool looks and hauntingly pale eyes, was the warmth and caring, the understanding heart that had been missing from his life.

He had dreamed a man's dream for years now, had believed that someday he would have again all that he'd lost. Imagining came easily to him. Even now he imagined that the warmer look in Kate's eyes and the gentleness in her touch would always be there for him. Only they came in the wake of another emotion—one he'd never use to his advantage. At some other time, when sympathy hadn't made her vulnerable to him, he would say the words that expressed what he'd begun to feel for her. But not now, not at this precise moment, when her lips were only a hairbreadth from his. Not when he felt them pressing softly, willingly against his cheek.

He felt the need for her claw at him and placed a wispy kiss upon her eyebrow. He held her loosely to him as a friend would, but knew he was feeling again. Living. And loving? It was a breath away.

Chapter Six

Sunlight glared off the windows of Kate's car as she drove toward the bank and tried to make sense of her own feelings. Had Saturday evening been a dream? Had she really been pressing herself against him, reaching out to give tenderness, to receive it again? She needed order in her life, wanted predictability and throve on common sense. All of those considerations had been tossed aside during those few moments.

He'd revealed a different side that had eclipsed all the reasons Kate had drummed up not to get involved with him. She'd believed that Tony was shallower, less aware, more selfish. Yet when he'd talked about his wife and child, she'd seen a depth of caring in his brooding eyes, had heard the anguish he'd suffered.

Now, in the light of day, common sense and feelings warred within her. How could what she'd believed before be true? He'd faced tragedy. He'd experienced the ultimate loss and had fought back.

Her brain was muddled. She wanted to cling to the man he seemed to be, who made her blood hum when he touched her. She couldn't think straight or logically. She couldn't think at all when around him.

By lunchtime she needed quiet more than anything else. She slipped out to her favorite restaurant and was seated at a small table for two in the tearoom, which was mostly patronized by women. Poking at her salad, Kate couldn't recall ever seeing a man there before.

As she spotted a certain dark-haired one at a table across the room, she froze, holding a shrimp in midair on the tines of her fork.

Smiling, Tony raised a bite-sized watercress sandwich to her in salute. It looked incongruous in his large hand.

Kate lowered her hand, stifled a laugh behind her napkin and sensed she was in big trouble.

At eight on Tuesday evening she stood at an ironing board, listening to Patsy Cline wail about her lover's cheating heart, while a hamburger sizzled in a frying pan. Kate stepped away to slide the meat patty onto a plate. As she shifted from the stove toward the sink, water slopped beneath her feet.

Dreading to look, she lowered her head slowly and stared at the water oozing its way from under the sink cabinet. Kate squatted and whipped open the doors. Water squirted at her. Cursing, she rushed to the linen closet to grab towels.

Cradling an armful, she was hurrying back when the bell rang. Soaked and in no mood to talk to a solicitor, she flung the door open. "I don't want to buy...." She fell silent at the sight of Tony's smile.

"I'm not selling."

Kate noticed the familiar glint of amusement in his gaze and said sharply, "Don't smile."

"What happened?" he asked, putting on a serious face and flicking his eyes to the dripping strands of her hair.

"A leaky pipe happened, so I don't have time—"

He dumped a box into her arms and brushed past. Kate stared at his back, at the box, and again at him.

By the time she reached the kitchen, his sneakers and socks had been dropped into a dry corner near the table. She leaned against the refrigerator and stared at the male body lying on the floor, head under the sink. Kate listened to his whistling while she scanned the muscular, denim-clad legs. She was in serious trouble, she reflected, feeling desire prick at her. "You don't have to..." she started, then stopped. If he wouldn't listen to her about anything else, why would he pay attention to her now? she reasoned, and plopped onto the closest chair. Dropping the towels, she stared at the box in her hands. It was heavy and square in shape. "What is in this box?"

When he didn't answer, she stepped over one of his legs and leaned forward to see his face. "What's in the box?" she repeated.

"It's for you. Open it," he called back as metal clanged against metal.

Kate squatted beside him and pried it open, wincing at the lusty curses he released every few moments. He muttered another, just as she removed the lid. A laugh rose into her throat. "How did you know?" she asked over the clang of the wrench, trying to see his face.

"Know what?"

Though his words were muffled, she could hear them. She stared down at the box of Tootsie Rolls. "How did you know that I love these things?"

"Wrappers in your office wastebasket," he said, twisting the wrench between grunts.

Kate felt her resolve crumbling. He was too observant. Gary hadn't realized her affinity for Tootsie Rolls until after they were married.

She heard another curse, a final one it seemed. Seconds later he placed his hands on the sink cabinet to pull himself back.

When his head popped out, Kate met him with a smile and motioned toward the sink. "How can I thank you?"

The towel that he'd snagged from the table masked everything but his eyes; they sparkled, then shifted to look back at the pipes. "There's no guarantee that I fixed it."

"Oh, it's fixed," she assured him lightly. "It wouldn't dare leak after what you said to it."

He laughed softly at her teasing and ran the towel over his damp forearms. "Then at the moment—" he paused and let his eyes stray to her lips "—at the moment a cup of coffee would do."

Kate struggled, as she'd struggled since they'd first met, to keep her feelings from going wild. Her mind screamed, *Run!* But she wasn't certain anymore if she wanted to run from him or into his arms. Cursing her weakness, she rushed away to pour him a cup of coffee.

"You won't always be able to avoid this by running, Kate."

Kate's shoulders sagged. He was always one step ahead of her. She wanted to sound steady and in control, but her pulse mocked her, racing at an uneven pace. "I'm not."

As she offered a cup, he folded his hand over hers, forcing her to stand still. "I've kissed you, and your lips spoke a different message to me. You want what I want."

"Tony, I can't get involved with you," she said, a touch panicky. "I made one mistake already. I can't do it again." Kate dodged eye contact with him. She'd said more than she'd planned to, but as he continued to stand firmly in her path, she reasoned that explanations might simplify her life. "I wouldn't have in the first place, if I had paid more attention to my mother's mistakes. Stupidly I married a man like my real father. Gary was a handsome, glib man. He romanced me, married me, and foolishly I worked while he played. He gave me bills that I paid while he pursued some fantasy to build the best racing car in the world. When he didn't succeed at that, he decided to sign up with a racing crew headed for Le Mans—without me. It didn't matter," she assured him in response to his quick-forming frown. "The marriage was already over."

His eyes, dark and searching, remained on her face. "Why did you help him, Kate?"

She drew a hard breath, wishing he weren't quite so perceptive.

"Did you believe in his dream?"

"Yes, I did." She swallowed her pride. "In the beginning I did." Nervously she crossed her arms. "Even when he'd invested every extra dime that I'd made and had begun to lose interest in building the racing car, I blinded myself to his shortcomings until I was forced to face them." She looked away; his stare told her he was deciphering too much. "When the marriage ended, I was determined never again to pin my hopes on any man who wasn't settled, who didn't have firm goals."

Reaching for her hand, Tony settled back and perched on the edge of the table. Protective instincts surfaced, even though he didn't know why he felt them. He sensed a quiet strength in her and couldn't understand why such a spirited woman would let one man affect her so much.

A little breathless, Kate uttered an appeal. "Tony, I can't deny that you're charming in an odd sort of way."

He broke into a short, quick laugh. "Your compliment could go to my head."

"I know about charming, handsome men," she responded, slipping her hand from his and leaning back against the refrigerator.

He took a hearty sip of the coffee, as if stalling. "What about fairness?" he asked. "Do you know about it, too?"

"Fairness?"

At her puzzled look, he wondered how she could even ask the question. Didn't she know what she was doing to him? Turning, he set the cup upon the table. Pushing to his feet, he stood in her path. "Does it seem right that I can't stop thinking about you, haven't been able to since the moment I walked into the neat cubicle you call an office?"

Her heart pumped a touch quicker. She'd heard a huskiness in his voice that made her think of intimacy. That made her shiver, yet warmed her, too. With his closeness, his breath fluttering across her face, desire stormed her again. Once again she wanted him to kiss her, to hold her. Instead, with a touch so light that she barely felt it, he skimmed her arm.

"I'll call you tomorrow," he said with the unwavering firmness that was by now familiar.

Kate searched for something to say, but her mind was blank. She felt a surrender taking place within her.

Let go, she thought—take the chance, but her stomach knotted in silent warning. With an unsettling feeling she watched him stride away. It was one she'd known before, one she wanted to shove aside, but suddenly couldn't. She knew the door had closed behind him, but all she could hear were his last words. She frowned, confused, and wondered if she dare take the chance with him that she wanted to take, the one he knew she wanted to take.

It was unbearably hot at eight the next morning. Kate ambled into her office, not believing the kind of evening she'd had. In the sedate quietness of the bank she would feel again some of the control over her life that she needed for peace of mind.

Five minutes later she learned that she was wrong. Hunched over her desk, she studied a profit and loss statement. At the click of footsteps outside her door, she raised her head to see a man in the brown uniform of a delivery service.

"Katherine Elliot." Head down, he kept his eyes riveted to the sheet on his clipboard. "For you," he announced, then set a huge white box in the middle of her desk. "Sign here."

Kate followed the finger that he tapped at the sheet of paper while she eyed the box. Frowning, she touched the string wrapped around it. "Who is it from?" she asked, looking up, but the man had disappeared as quickly as he'd arrived.

Scissors in hand, Kate clipped the string and pulled it from the box. Thinking the messenger had gone unnoticed, she found she was wrong for the second time.

Peeking around the corner of the doorway, Joanna grinned and inquired, "Who's it from?"

Kate merely shook her head, too stunned to offer a response. She lifted off the lid.

Joanna didn't move from the doorway. "What is it?" she wanted to know, curiosity coloring her voice.

Kate nudged aside the white tissue paper and just stared. No card was needed. Reaching in, she carefully lifted the carousel music box and placed it upon her desk. With a twist of the wind-up key, the strains of "The Carousel Waltz" filled her office. Brightly colored horses slowly revolved on the stand beneath a bright red scalloped canopy. Crazy. He was crazy. So was she. She couldn't forget him. He wouldn't let her.

"I like his style," Joanna said with an audible hint of admiration.

While Kate's head was screaming about the need for self-preservation, her heart cried out for love. She knew her heart was winning as she wondered what kind of man understood that flowers wouldn't have impressed her, that the usual gifts would have been enjoyed for a moment, then forgotten. But this, she mused, running a hand admiringly over the exquisite lines of the scalloped dome, this would go home with her, would be near for her to see all the time, would remind her of him constantly.

Joanna sighed exaggeratedly, apparently trying to gain Kate's attention. "Ah, a Prince Charming does exist."

Though twinges of pleasure rippled through her, Kate sent her friend a skeptical look.

"I'm sure you didn't buy that for yourself. A gift from the amusement park man? The charmer?"

Attempting to quell her own excitement, Kate wagged her head slowly at Joanna's teasing tone.

"That's encouraging." Joanna remained in the doorway. "I thought only frogs inhabited the earth."

Kate raised her eyes. "And you've changed your mind?"

"I may have oversimplified." Joanna gestured toward the carousel. "There may be a few knights, even a Prince Charming or two still in existence."

"What about the chinks in their armor?" Kate asked, looking to her friend to give her a reason to stay away from Tony.

Joanna wrinkled her nose. "I don't want to be too logical right now," she answered. "I met someone at the health club. His biceps are more impressive than his IQ, but I'm tired of conversing anyway."

Kate sighed in resignation. Joanna wouldn't offer her any help. "So the attorney is gone?"

"Off to court..." She paused and laughed at her own pun. "Off to court another," she finished, glancing at the clock that was ticking off the seconds before the bank opened to the public. "Talk later." She waved goodbye. "And I expect to hear *all*."

Kate stared at the carousel for a moment longer, then reached down to set the box under her desk.

Straightening, she pushed back her chair to retrieve a file folder that she'd nudged to the floor with her elbow. With a quick sweep of her hand, she plucked it up, then jumped as the telephone rang. Even before she reached for the receiver, she knew who was calling.

Tony didn't wait for a formal greeting. "Do you like it?" he asked.

She sighed, feeling herself slipping another notch. "It's beautiful. Thank you. But you shouldn't be sending me gifts."

"Why not?"

She cradled the receiver between her jaw and shoulder. Why not? His words echoed at her. Kate curled the telephone cord around her finger. Why couldn't he be just a pleasant memory in her life, if she expected nothing more? If she didn't look for promises this time, if she expected nothing, then why not?

"I'll pick you up at seven tonight."

"Tony—"

"You're going to the gallery, aren't you?"

She released a long, not too steady breath and felt youthful anticipation rippling through her. "You're complicating everything."

"An evening at the art gallery, Kate. I'm only asking for a few hours."

No, he was asking for much more. She suspected he was smiling at that moment, waiting patiently for her answer. His patience seemed her undoing.

"Your silence means yes?"

She struggled to stifle a laugh and made a Herculean effort to say one word. "No."

"Kate, Kate, Kate," he said softly. "What shall we do?"

"I don't know what you're going to do," she said, smiling. "But I'm going to say goodbye now."

"Till later," he responded.

Kate opened her mouth to contradict him, but heard instead the click of the receiver.

Impossible. The man was incredibly stubborn. He didn't know how to take no for an answer, and she wasn't certain she could go on saying it to him.

Too many feelings that she'd smothered since her divorce suddenly seemed close at hand. It had been unreasonable to believe the hormones of a thirty-year-old woman would not get in the way occasionally, but she wasn't prepared to allow desire to run her life. All she had to do was rationalize her feelings. She was attracted to him. He made her want to laugh. He made her feel young and vulnerable again. Could she enjoy that part of the relationship and keep her heart protected?

By five that afternoon, Tony had polished his shoes and slipped his tuxedo out of the cleaner's bag. He'd finished snapping on the cummerbund, but the tie still dangled from his opened collar. He was also up to his elbow in diapers. "How could one little girl need so many of these things?" he murmured as he finished snapping up his niece's terry-cloth sleeper.

Belly up on a blanket in the middle of the living room, Sara cooed back at him.

He plopped onto the sofa, exhausted. He'd forgotten how much work someone so small was. Relaxing for the first time since he'd entered his sister's house an hour and a half ago, he glanced around.

With its stark black-and-white decor, teardrop chandeliers and walls of mirrors, the home was more his brother-in-law's than his sister's. Teresa's warmth wasn't present, and looking down at Sara, who lived in the cozy nursery, a cocoon of pink and white on the second floor, Tony wondered if she would ever feel the warmth and laughter that Teresa and he had known while growing up.

Leaning forward, he lifted Sara onto his lap. She raised enormous dark eyes at him and smiled. His sister would claim that the baby had grimaced from a gas bubble. Tony knew better. Sara had smiled at him. He had a way with the ladies—though one of them was becoming a bit of a challenge.

Bending his head, he kissed the silky strands of Sara's dark hair and inhaled her sweet smell. She already knew the way to her uncle's heart. She also nudged at the old ache, the twinge that at one time had promised to destroy him whenever he thought of his own son. He needed this, he realized, cuddling her closer.

He was a man who'd always thought life wasn't complete without a wife and a family. But wanting something didn't mean that a person would find it. He'd never really expected to—until now. Kate was making him believe in dreams again—real dreams.

Glancing at the clock, Kate swept her hair away from her face and secured it with pearl combs. When Tony had called back, she'd said yes. She'd said it so naturally that she'd felt panic the minute she set down the telephone receiver. Restless now, she rushed back to the closet and grabbed a plain white silk dress with thin straps and a matching jacket.

At three minutes after seven, a flash of lights from a car shone through her bedroom window. Nervous again, she rushed to it, feeling just like she had before her first prom. She was regressing to her teens, she thought disgustedly, zipping up her dress. If she wasn't careful, she'd begin acting like a ninny.

The headlights dimmed; Kate saw that they were those of a Porsche, not Tony's beat-up-looking truck. As the car door opened, Kate caught herself gaping at him.

She whipped away from the window to hunt for a pair of her favorite earrings, teardrop pearls. Nerves scrambled again. She was excited, looking forward to the evening with him. She tried to remember that Prince Charming didn't exist, didn't suddenly materialize in the real life of a rather ordinary woman named Katherine Elliot. That last reminder disintegrated when she opened the door, when her eyes met his, when he winked at her in appreciation.

Soft music and a buzz of conversation greeted them when they entered the gallery. It was small but had two exhibition rooms, one on the first floor and another five steps up. Kate had helped her mother redecorate the interior with track lights strategically placed in archways, nooks and alcoves. While her mother was displaying many of her own works, she'd wisely shared the spotlight with several equally talented but lesser-known photographers and painters.

As her mother breezed past people and weaved her way to Kate, she called a greeting across the room.

"Nervous?" Kate asked, hugging her, and knew the answer by her mother's tight embrace.

"Enormously." Claire stepped back and placed a well-manicured hand at her midsection. "Queasy stomach. Sweaty palms. The whole works."

"Take it easy," Tony soothed, stepping around Kate and squeezing Claire's hand. His simple advice seemed to help. Her mother's lips curved into a genuine smile before he strolled toward the makeshift bar.

"You're surrounded by friends," Kate assured her, realizing that Tony's relationship with her mother had grown into a sturdy friendship.

"I'm glad you decided to date Tony."

Claire also never gave up, Kate had to admit, leaning back against the wall and noticing that the loud-talking Texan Larry Wilkins had arrived in a Bola tie at the black-tie affair. "It's not really a date."

"It could be the beginning of something wonderful."

Kate couldn't help but smile. Her mother heard only herself when she wanted to, so although she was smart, she often came across as an inhabitant of La-La land. Ignoring her comment, Kate brushed her mother's cheek with a kiss. "I'm glad the opening is such a success."

Claire nodded, her eyes darting around the room. "I suppose it won't be if I don't get another platter of stuffed mushrooms on the buffet table. People are more amiable when free eats are involved."

"It is a success. And you mingle. I'll take care of the buffet table."

"Thank you, dear. I'd probably drop the platter, and then everyone would know what a nervous wreck I really am."

Kate took only two steps, then her smile faded.

Standing near the buffet, Tony snugly held the waist of a tall, dark-haired woman in a red dress. Bending close to hear her speak, his intimate stance conveyed the message that they'd shared a lot of history.

Kate whipped around and stared so hard at the photograph before her, a silhouette of a young girl, sunlight slanting across her fair hair, that the picture blurred.

She told herself that she didn't care if he cuddled up with a hundred different women. But was it more than pride that insisted he not do it when he was on a date with her? If he didn't matter to her, why did she suddenly feel like taking a poke at him?

Wineglasses in his hands, Tony assured his sister that he would introduce her to Claire Vesterhal's daughter. While he inched his way back to Kate, he couldn't shake his concern for Teresa. She had put on a good act, but he'd seen the strain between her and his brother-in-law minutes ago. Trouble seemed close at hand.

He was halfway across the room when Claire stepped into his path. "You managed a giant step tonight."

He grinned. "So did you," he said, gesturing with his head toward more guests who were straggling in.

"I'm not that great," she said without hesitation. "I've been lucky. You, too." She glanced at her daughter. "Kate was wonderfully photogenic for me to practice on."

"Not prejudiced, are you?"

"A teensy bit," she admitted unabashedly. "Someday I'll have to show you the photographs that I have from her childhood. In one," she went on, "she put on my best heels. She couldn't have been more than five. We didn't have much then, just the two of us. She was pretending to be a princess and..." Her voice faded, her eyes brightening with an impish sparkle. "Oh, I do run on, don't I? Why didn't you stop me?"

Tony kissed her cheek. "I never tire of your stories, Claire."

"Or of hearing about my daughter?" she teased.

As he watched her glide forward to join a couple that was eyeing one of the paintings, amusement flickered inside him. He had a valuable ally. A smart one.

She was right. He couldn't seem to get enough of her daughter. The idea that she'd become so important in such a short amount of time rocked him. He couldn't say when he'd begun to feel so much for her. But during the moments while he'd watched her courageously picking her way through the remains of her mother's home to find treasures of the heart, he'd felt that he'd just gained one more of his own.

Quickly he made his way toward her.

The evening couldn't get worse, Kate thought. She eyed the man with a turquoise pinkie ring devouring the cheese puffs and turned to step away. She stood eye to eye with Tony. Right behind him was the dark-haired vision in the red dress.

Smiling, the vision floated toward them. "I thought Tony might forget his promise to introduce us."

Kate didn't plan on playing the other woman's game. She took a step. Only one.

"I'm his sister," the beauty said, smiling even more warmly . "Teresa."

"Sister?" Kate murmured, praying that she wasn't gaping, but as Tony handed her the wineglass, she saw too much amusement in his eyes to believe her surprise had passed unnoticed.

"Your mother will be a huge success," Teresa went on.

Kate nodded a thank-you with a tight-lipped smile, aware she'd already come close to jamming her foot into her mouth.

"I heard that you were at Luigi's the other night, but you didn't get a chance to eat there." Teresa said the words lightly, the tease in her eyes directed at her brother. "Papa's planning on more restaurants, maybe even one in California."

"Onward and upward," Tony quipped.

His sister's responding laugh lasted for only a second.

"Your father was lucky," a blond-haired man cut in. "A peasant from Italy with nothing more than a few recipes in his back pocket couldn't become so successful so quickly today," he said with a sarcastic smirk.

"He worked hard," Tony retorted. "Damn hard."

Tension thickened. As Tony introduced his brother-in-law to Kate, Jon Harmon seemed more intent on rattling Teresa. Kate watched her draw a shaky breath even while she sent Kate a quick smile.

When Jon turned away, Teresa said by way of excuse, "He's had a little too much to drink."

Tony didn't look convinced. "What's his excuse other times?"

"Tony," Teresa said in an appealing voice. Her fingers noticeably tightened on the stem of her glass while she struggled to hold on to a smile for Kate. "Papa has worked hard. He did start out with a few family recipes, a dishwasher—"

"That was me," Tony reminded her.

His sister responded to his deliberate lightness with a laugh, but it died when she nervously looked back at her husband. "I'd better go."

Tony matched her frown. "See you, kiddo." Eyes on his brother-in-law, he shook his head slowly. "No appreciation."

Simple words that spoke volumes, Kate mused, noticing that the man with the Indian jewelry had gobbled up the last cheese puff on the buffet table.

"Got a thing for him?" Tony teased, brushing a knuckle across her cheek.

Kate heard humor in his voice but couldn't ignore a serious thought. "He might be safer."

"Is that what you want?"

"I don't want to make more mistakes," she said honestly. In a rush to get away from her own thoughts as much as from him, she took a step back. "I promised to get more food."

He nodded. "I'll wait. I'm not going anywhere without you."

Kate took a step, then paused in midstride and glanced back at him. She couldn't recall any man ever saying that to her before—not even Gary. After the divorce she'd blamed herself for expecting to hear it, had made herself come to terms with expectations that had apparently been too high.

It was nonsense to take Tony's words to heart. But she was sentimental, a romantic, even. Logic faded when she was around him, because he kept saying or doing something that prevented her from pigeonholing him. No matter how much she tried, she couldn't push him into the slot where she'd filed her ex-husband.

Annoyed by her own confusion, she scurried into her mother's office for the caterer's platter. She nearly rocked back on her heels at the sight of Jimmy Foster perched on a table. "What are you doing here?"

He munched on the stuffed mushroom cradled between his thumb and finger. "I work here now."

Not for the first time, she thought that he was trouble. She swept past him to pick up the platter of food that he'd been sampling. "Then you'd better do that, hadn't you?"

He grinned at her, and she felt his gaze drift down from her face toward her breasts. "I was hungry."

Panic fluttered briefly in Kate's stomach. Tightening her grip on the platter, she whirled around, but his hand shot out. The viselike grip on her wrist nearly shook the tray from her grasp, and only the faint buzz of voices from the other room kept her calm. She wasn't alone. More angry than afraid, Kate glanced down, knowing she could use the platter as a weapon if she had to. She could also scream. But wouldn't that make a nice little headline for her mother's gallery? "Take your hand off me," she demanded, stepping back in a small show of a struggle.

He seemed more inclined to scare than harm her. Smiling more broadly, he opened his fingers, releasing her wrist, then flashed his palm tauntingly close to her face.

Instinctively Kate reared back, then moved around him. As she rushed from the room toward the gallery, his laugh rang in her ears. Fuming, Kate set the platter upon the table and sought out her mother.

Snagging her arm as she passed, Kate ushered her to a quiet spot where they could talk privately. "Why did you hire Jimmy Foster?"

Looking dumbfounded at the question, Claire waved her hand in a carefree manner. "I needed help."

Seeing her mother glance distractedly toward a newspaper columnist, Kate gripped her arms and forced eye-to-eye contact. "Mother, you don't know anything about him."

"Well, that's not really true."

Kate tried to keep anxiety out of her voice. "What do you know about him except that he's Louisa's cook's son?"

"Louisa said he's had a difficult time. Prison and all."

Kate could barely keep her voice to a whisper as she insisted on hearing every fragment of information her mother had about him.

"He was having trouble finding a job," Claire added in a tone that indicated Kate should understand why he'd been hired. "You knew that."

Kate knew and still didn't understand why her mother had to be so gullible.

"Well, I talked to Tony and he—"

"Tony did what?" Kate dropped her hands to her sides.

"He'd hired men to help disassemble the rides at the amusement park, and some of them had questionable pasts."

"So you relied on Tony's judgment," she said in disbelief.

"He obviously believes as I do. People deserve a second chance."

Kate seethed.

"We can't hold someone's past mistakes against them forever, Katie," her mother said in a low voice, zeroing in again on the woman from the arts and leisure section of the local newspaper.

Kate wanted to pounce on Claire, make her think clearly. But she merrily accepted the columnist's undivided attention and rambled on about the gray shadows that ran like sensuous rivers across the roof of a building in one photograph.

"So serene," the columnist chirped.

Kate should have felt relief; the first uncertain moments of the opening were over and her mother obviously had the snotty reviewer's favorable eye. But nothing felt serene, especially her stomach, which was protesting the wine she'd drunk earlier. Her mother wasn't thinking. And Tony hadn't helped one iota.

"Is something wrong?"

Kate whipped around to face him. "More than wrong." Illogically or not, she blamed him. "This is your fault."

Tony frowned. One step forward, two back. What had he done now? Puzzled, he tipped his head slightly to see her expression. It was somber, pained. "Maybe we should leave so you can tell me what I'm guilty of doing."

"I'm leaving. Alone," she snapped.

"No, you're not," he said quietly, but with a firmness that allowed for no opposition.

She whirled away. Frustration mingled with worry, even panic, for her mother.

Tony caught up with her and lightly touched her arm to guide her toward the door. "Let's step outside before your mother sees how upset you are."

"She knows how upset I am." Kate tugged her arm from his grip and marched forward, preceding him into the night air and away from the guests.

Chapter Seven

A step behind her when she halted and whirled to face him, Tony reared abruptly to prevent himself from plowing into her. "Okay. What's going on?"

A warm breeze curled around Kate, but didn't cool her fury. "She's hired a criminal to help her." She saw his eyes narrow in the manner of someone trying to decipher a foreign language.

"An ex-convict—Edith Foster's son," Kate said as he continued to stare at her uncomprehendingly.

"He's not a hardened ex-con." His brows drew together. "He's just a kid. Nineteen."

He responded with so little concern that she wanted to kick some sense into him. "He's a man," Kate countered. "And he spent the last year in jail. Car

theft, from what I've pieced together. But what he did
isn't important here. My mother feels confident that
he's okay because you hired ex-convicts. My mother
has lost her home and two husbands, and now you
make her vulnerable to losing all she has left. Your
attitude is very commendable but a bit unrealistic.
You've made her believe that she can trust any of
them."

"Whoa." He raised a hand to halt her. "What
Claire does isn't my business."

"Exactly," she retorted. "Thank you for being so
helpful and wise after the fact. But if you truly cared,
then you'd have reasoned with her. She could be in
danger." She wanted to scream at Tony that Jimmy
was dangerous, but Kate wasn't absolutely certain if
he would make a threatening move to anyone but herself.

Tony didn't miss the distress still heavily lacing her
voice. "Did something happen?"

She wrestled with herself for calm. Stupid. She was
revealing too much, allowing a closeness with a man
that she'd learned was destructive. She took a deep
breath. To say more might mean cringing with regret
later. She was being unfair. Without knowing about
the incident she'd experienced with Jimmy, Tony
couldn't understand her alarm. "She receives works of
other artists on consignment. Some of it is too valuable to be in the hands of a man with a streak of lar-
ceny in his veins."

Though she sounded more reasonable now, he cupped a hand at the nape of her neck and persisted. "What happened?"

Kate looked away. He was more sensitive than she'd expected. Judging by the curtness of his voice, he'd also been raised with some macho values, including one that would insist he defend a woman's honor. Again she considered how damaging a scene would be for her mother's gallery. "Words. I had words with him. He was nibbling at the food platter."

He sent her a puzzled look.

"Forget it," she urged.

Her request wasn't easy for him. Only an insensitive clod wouldn't recognize that something more serious than a pilfered mushroom had caused such agitation in her.

He wasn't sure about the surly-looking kid. He'd met his share of Jimmy Foster types—angry and lazy. Though Tony stretched to give people the benefit of the doubt, the Foster kid fitted that description. Tony's agreement with Claire had stemmed from personal circumstances. He'd endured too much personal tragedy not to believe, not to need something as motivating as the idea of a second chance. He believed in them. He'd had to for his own sanity. And he believed that meant finding the right woman again—one like the person standing before him.

As he saw her chin rise, he knew better than to prod too much. "I'll keep an eye on her." His words carried more than that simple message. He'd keep an eye on Kate, too. She needed someone who understood just how gentle a soul she was. They'd both lost, but he had memories filled with joy. Her memories of her marriage had obviously left a bitter taste in her mouth. She'd both given and lost a part of herself. Though she possessed a strong spirit, she seemed to have an incredibly soft heart. He would never hurt her. In time she would learn that.

Kate started to turn away, but he leaned closer, stopping her. With his breath, warm and sweet, fanning her face, she knew something had happened between them despite her certainty that nothing was going on. She didn't want this, she told herself. She'd given up dreaming about this kind of excitement, hadn't she? She didn't want some man in her life who shifted the ground beneath her with every touch, every kiss. She didn't want a lot of things, she thought, but couldn't draw back.

Weary of her own anger, she couldn't fight the anticipation of something as old as time rushing through her. He inched so close that she felt the sturdy hardness of his thighs against her.

Kate lowered her lashes and closed her eyes the instant his lips covered hers. The kiss wasn't gentle this time. It demanded she cling to him.

He took his fill of her and she gave in, tasting him. She had been yearning, wanting this again, even as she'd denied its existence. She heard a moan. Her own or his? She couldn't distinguish where the sound had begun any more than she could separate the mingling of their breath, the fusing of their lips, the blending of their bodies. Though it was nothing more than a kiss, it stunned her with its passion, with the raw desire that he aroused so effortlessly within her.

She was stepping over the edge again, wandering toward that old dream, the one she'd discarded with excruciating pain when her marriage had ended, when she'd realized that life didn't bring all that a person hoped for. And she was facing fear again.

"This is crazy," she murmured against his mouth. She wanted to step back, to escape, but he seemed unwilling to release her.

He held his arm firmly against her back and lightly ran a fingertip across her swollen lips. She couldn't speak. She was accepting his offering, but knew that an explosion might follow. It could devastate the safe world she'd erected for herself. She really didn't want to be charmed and especially didn't want to fall in love.

Tony felt her tense a second before he pushed back. There was no anger. Just pain. Distrust. Quick and fleeting, the emotions shadowed her eyes, then slipped away as she regained the control that she seemed so determined to hang on to.

He wanted to feel her in his arms again, wanted to stir the warmth that he'd only sampled. He wanted her.

He understood his own physical needs. He was too old not to. But how could he explain that lust only grazed the surface of what she stirred within him?

He would wait. He'd been waiting for what seemed like an eternity to fill the void in his heart. He'd even thought that it might never happen. Now he knew differently.

The emptiness would go away.

All through Thursday, Kate didn't allow herself to think about anything but work. Evening proved the most difficult time. Determined not to think about him, she spent hours cleaning her apartment. Before she went to bed, her apartment gleamed, and her furniture could have passed a "white glove" inspection.

In the morning she abandoned her usual half hour of savoring coffee while thumbing through the newspaper. To sit still anywhere for too long meant having time to think.

Out of sorts, she trudged toward the bank an hour later. With each step she took, more perspiration soaked her linen jacket. Raising a handkerchief to her face to blot dots of moisture from her upper lip, she glanced up at the sky. Sultry heat had smothered whatever fresh air there might have been. In the distance, dark clouds hung low and rolled slowly toward the city. Rain would end the blaze that had raged for days in the woods. Rain would make the heat even more unbearable, she thought, welcoming the coolness of the air-conditioned bank as the doors closed behind her.

In passing, she waved to Joanna. Standing in her teller's cage, Joanna wiggled her fingers in return and continued counting the money for her cash drawer.

Kate's attempts to stick to a schedule failed consistently. Late that afternoon she finally tucked a new plan for an insurance policy on Tony's property under her arm and approached her supervisor.

After several minutes, nothing was going as she'd hoped it would, and the humorless Edgar Svenson looked even more foreboding than usual. Kate watched the right corner of his mouth twitch. From experience she'd learned that was a telltale sign of an impending scowl.

"Your approval of this loan puzzles me," he said, as she'd anticipated.

"Mr. Svenson, with the additional insurance coverage, the property is no longer a high-risk venture."

"But it is prime fire property. And his insurance coverage right now is inadequate. What guarantee do you have that he won't drop the additional coverage once the loan is approved?"

Guarantee? Could she give any kind of a guarantee as far as Tony was concerned?

"In the past you were more levelheaded. In the past you've shown a clear-cut approach to issuing loans."

In the past she hadn't known Tony.

"Why would you encourage the issuance of such a loan?"

Good question, Kate conceded. "I feel that Mr. Patelli's business is a good investment."

Mr. Svenson eyed the report before him and frowned again. "I shall have to make that decision," he said in the pompous tone that never failed to make Kate grit her teeth. "Set up an appointment. I'll meet with Mr. Patelli and then I'll make a decision. At present, Ms. Elliot, the man has little collateral to back up a loan of this magnitude."

Kate arranged an appointment for Tony with the formidable Edgar Svenson, then left his office. But she wasn't too hopeful. She placed a phone call to get the results of the review of Tony's financial credibility, praying he hadn't written a bad check or overloaded a credit-card account.

The day really wasn't going well. And the computers were down.

With a glance at the clock, she pushed back her chair and rounded her desk to get a cup of coffee before she left for the day.

Uncharacteristically her supervisor wasn't rushing around the bank wearing that pedantic scowl of his and peering over co-workers' shoulders to see what they were up to.

Mr. Svenson stood as if frozen, his back against the wall. Kate scanned the bank-tellers' area. A young woman was tugging her two-year-old son toward the exit while juggling several department-store bags, and tellers were smiling at customers and exchanging cash. Everyone was behaving normally—all of them except Joanna.

Pale, she stared fixedly at the man standing at her window. Kate dragged in a breath, unable to move or speak, her eyes riveted on the gun barrel peeking from the bottom of his jacket. While Joanna piled money into a bag as if stuffing a turkey, Kate's mind raced. She touched Mr. Svenson's arm lightly, but he jerked as if stung. Kate opened her mouth but no words came out. Nowhere in her neat, orderly life had she allowed for a bank robbery.

She didn't give herself a moment to think beyond the next one. Praying silently that she wouldn't be noticed, she inched back into her office. The moment she reached its safety, she spun around. One foot slipped beneath her. Winded, her heart pounding, she grabbed at the edge of the desk, straightened and stamped her foot on the silent button near her chair.

Tony stepped from his car and stared at the bank. He'd debated most of the day about pushing Kate. Then a half hour ago, he'd had an attack of missing Kate. He needed to hear her voice, to see her smile.

Dodging cars, he dashed across the street. On the sidewalk outside the bank, a child tugged away from his mother and plopped his fanny onto the concrete, plainly hell-bent on throwing a temper tantrum.

Striding hurriedly to the double glass doors, Tony hit one with the palm of his hand and winced at the sight of the man who suddenly appeared on the other side of the glass. Through it, Tony watched him fly backward. Off balance, he flailed his arms, then hit the ground, backside first, the bag in his hand sliding across the gleaming floor. In seemingly slow motion action played out before Tony's eyes, a security guard rushed forward, gun drawn. Sirens howled. Tires screeched on the street behind Tony. Cops glanced at him as they ran past.

Fear rose into his throat. Tony didn't give himself time to fully consider his concern. He charged in, searching for Kate, and saw her standing beside another woman, a tall brunette who looked pale and shaken.

Sounds of chaos filled the bank. Kate didn't bother to look up. She heard the commotion and knew the police had arrived, guns drawn. Hugging Joanna, she offered soothing words. As her friend slumped onto a nearby chair to answer questions for a uniformed officer, Kate tried to scan the bank, but a wall of co-workers' backs blocked her view.

"Guess your bank has a hero," the officer said.

Her hand on Joanna's shoulder, Kate frowned in puzzlement. "What happened?"

"Some guy came in as the robber was rushing out. Clobbered him with the door," he said with a short laugh.

Kate smiled and took a small step to see the hero. Nothing had prepared her for the sight of the starchy Edgar Svenson pumping Tony's hand.

* * *

"Why did you agree to have dinner with me?" Tony asked an hour later, opening the door to his home.

Kate couldn't resist a tease. "I've always had a thing for heroes."

He flushed slightly and looked away, as if amazed by his own reaction. "I'm no hero."

"Some people think you are." She caught his wink but was distracted. This was what Tony called home? He lived within walking distance of the amusement park in a building that resembled a garage-sized warehouse. When he'd slid open the wide drive-in door, she'd expected to feel the insufferable heat so common to storage sheds. Instead she'd been met by the coolness provided by an air-conditioning unit.

Sparsely decorated, the room resembled a health club. Kate eyed the barbells, bench press and the set of gymnast's rings dangling from the ceiling.

"This way."

Turning, Kate caught him gesturing toward a door. Her curiosity piqued, she followed him into the next room. It was a pleasant surprise. Walls had been finished, floors had been planked, soft cushiony furniture filled the space. It was cozy and intimate and soon glowed with the warmth of the candles he lighted one at a time.

Kate heard the clatter of pots and turned toward the sound. The kitchen, painted a soft yellow with shiny copper-bottomed pots hanging overhead, was definitely a haven for someone who liked to cook.

While Tony rummaged in the refrigerator, Kate settled onto a bar stool near the telephone and sipped the iced tea that he poured for her. Swiveling the stool, she noted the pine table and chairs by one window. But at the sight of a hammock strung in a corner, she couldn't help but laugh. His decor was a far cry from the mauve furnishings and sleek, sophisticated furniture in her own apartment. "We really are different," she murmured, more to herself than to him.

"Thankfully." She heard the amusement in his voice.

Kate strove for a more serious sound. "Opposites don't really attract, Tony."

Palming a head of lettuce, he frowned. "Who said?"

Kate swiveled again to face him squarely. "I said."

He stood before the stove, carrots dangling from one hand, the lettuce in his other. "One isn't a majority."

Kate geared up for a challenge. Though she'd always preferred quiet relationships, she was beginning to enjoy sparring with him. "What is?"

"Two. Convince me with facts. You believe in facts, don't you?"

She bent her head and hid a smile while she sipped her iced tea. "And then?"

"Then I might agree."

She really doubted that he easily changed his mind about anything. Looking dubiously over her shoulder, she slid off the stool and strolled toward the hammock. "No arguments, then?"

"All you have to do is prove you're right."

Kate dropped her shoulder bag onto the hammock. She suddenly didn't feel so determined to prove that they were wrong for each other. If they were, why did it feel so right to be with him? "We don't even think the same way," she started. "You owned a successful restaurant, which you sold because you tired of it."

Taking a relaxed stance, he leaned back against the refrigerator. "I didn't tire of it."

As she looked up, she saw the appeal in his eyes for her to understand.

"I needed something different, something I'd have to work hard at," he went on. "Something that I knew would bring fun into my life. So I bought the amusement park."

Kate realized that she hadn't been fair to him when they'd first met. She'd had a great many misconceptions. Ghosts from her past? she wondered, looking down and pushing a heel against the floor. The hammock swayed gently beneath her.

She set one foot firmly upon the floor. "I thought that I had my life well planned," she said abruptly.

Shifting his shoulder, he pushed away from the refrigerator. "And?"

"And suddenly I find that I have a problem." She didn't want to get hurt. How could she explain that? "Tony, you're my problem."

He saw confusion in her eyes. "Why?"

"You're carefree. I'm structured. I like security. I like—" As he closed the distance between them, her heart began to thud.

Silently, his eyes never leaving hers, he squatted before her and framed her face with his hands. "I'm crazy about you, Kate."

She felt her insides turn to mush. Nothing felt steady. Not her breathing, her pulse, nor her heart. "You don't make this easy."

"*You* don't." Tony wanted to tell her that he understood what it was like to hurt. He'd thought he would never smile or laugh—hell, he'd thought he'd never feel anything again but agony. Yet here he was, ready to live again, really live. And dammit, if he had the guts to do it, then why shouldn't she? "What do you want me to do?" he asked softly.

A monumental question, Kate decided. "I don't know."

"Yes, you do." His voice softened to a caressing whisper. "You didn't come for dinner."

She closed her eyes, but couldn't block out her feelings for him. "No," she answered and sighed, knowing she was taking a step with him that she'd denied wanting. But slow and rumbling, desire had erupted every time they'd been together. She'd been dodging it uselessly.

"Why don't you stop analyzing this? Quit worrying about what-ifs?"

"That's not easy for me," she admitted. As his breath fanned her face, as his lips hovered near hers, she rushed on. "Don't expect miracles."

"But I do."

"I've been married, Tony, and—"

He caught a handful of her hair and gently drew it back to force her eyes to meet his. Smiling eyes—gentle eyes. "So have I," he murmured.

"It ended unhappily," Kate whispered, shivering beneath the sensuous trace of his tongue on her ear. He spirited away her objections. He made her want to believe in something she'd given up on long ago. He made her ache for the arms tightening around her and drawing her to stand with him.

"So did mine," he said softly, feeling her vulnerability and his own. He hadn't wanted any woman this much in what seemed like an eternity. He kissed her gently, but need drove him to take a deeper taste. To say he wasn't as vulnerable as she was would be a lie. Men quaked with their own uncertainties, and at the moment, he had plenty. He wanted to please her as much as himself. He wanted more than her body, but knew that was all she would offer him for the moment, all he could expect.

Kate leaned toward him and sighed at the caressing touch of his fingers.

"I want you." He spoke in a husky whisper against her cheek. "You want me. What else is important?"

What about tomorrow? she wanted to ask. But it was her last conscious thought. Suddenly only the moment mattered.

In the distance she heard the rumble of thunder, the promise of relief from the sweltering heat outside. Yet all she could think about was the warmth that was building up within her. As if under a spell, she found herself following the command of the hand that cupped the back of her neck. She clung, answering his kiss, absorbing his taste, wanting it. And wanting more, she realized, coiling her arms around his back. Touching, feeling, tasting. Emotion controlled her responses. She answered the urgency of the mouth on hers until she wanted to sag against him.

Pausing for breath, she tore her mouth from his and looked down to unbutton his shirt, but his lips wouldn't leave hers. They nibbled and savored while his shirt buttons opened beneath her hands. As if she were a creature of touch only, she closed her eyes and splayed her fingers, letting them slowly roam up the flat ripples of his stomach to his sturdy chest. "This is—"

"This is whatever you want it to be," he murmured softly, his fingers at the button on her skirt.

As it slithered to the floor, she knew she was baring more than her body to him. Vulnerable, she nonetheless stood still. Trustingly still.

His eyes on hers, warm and hooded, he searched her face while he unbuttoned her blouse, then slowly lifted one strap of her bra. She felt gentleness in his touch, in the kiss upon her shoulder, the brush of his lips as light as a butterfly's caress. As her bra hooks were unclasped, coolness whispered at her back, but no chill rippled over her. When he hooked his fingers into her panties and his mouth traced a slow, sensuous path across her belly, heat filled her. Stormed her.

Closing her eyes, Kate gave in to sensation, listening to the whisper of silk, willingly swaying beneath the stroke of his tongue. As reality slipped from her grasp, she gripped his shoulders tightly, fiercely. She wouldn't listen to her head anymore. If her heart suffered, then it would do so in grand style.

He murmured huskily against her throat, but she couldn't respond. She felt impatient, hungry as seconds passed like forever before they came together on the bed.

A fire for him burned within her. She reached for the snap of his jeans, tugging at them in her eagerness to caress him. She used her foot, touching his as they pushed together at the fabric, shoving it down. One second. Two. A breath taken. No more time was given before he shifted to free himself of his pants.

Kisses became hungrier, her mouth fastening onto his, while his hands skimmed her flesh. New. Everything was so new. Discovering everything was the force that drove them. She found herself gasping to keep pace with the madness, feeling her pulse pound as he caressed, as his hands and mouth blazed a trail from her breast to her belly and then lower. Excitement. Urgency. Heat. All whirled around her.

When he shifted again, she opened her eyes to the face above her, caught by slanting shadows and the moonlight streaming into the room. She lost herself in his eyes, dark and warm and passionate as they stared down at her. And she believed in fantasy. She believed all things were possible.

Breathless, she murmured his name, and as his hands slid beneath her hips, Kate raised them to him, urging him on. Gasping, she took him into her while she stroked the smooth planes of his face, the rough bristle of his jaw, the taut muscles in his shoulders, back and buttocks. And she coaxed him to lead her.

As she sighed, she heard him laugh softly, the sound of his pleasure echoing in her head. They rolled over the bed, locked together, bound by a merging as old as time. She felt the rapidity of his heartbeat against her chest, heard his ragged breathing blending with her own, felt the tension, power and hunger. Passion consumed them, swirling them into a mindless fantasy that didn't allow reality to enter. This was the place where dreams were made, where demands changed into promises, where desire mingled with love—a place she suddenly never wanted to leave.

Shuddering, clinging, she heard him whisper her name, a song in her ears, and began again to believe in those dreams.

Chapter Eight

Tony didn't move, couldn't for a long moment as he struggled to breathe. He'd burned for her. He'd trembled. Sensations had curled around him.

He lay still, waiting while his heartbeat slowly returned to some semblance of normalcy. Despite the mantle of darkness, he could see her face, soft in the afterglow of passion. He wanted to see it that way often, wanted to see her smile for him. He wanted to hear her laugh with him.

But now, with her snuggling close, her warmth a part of him, her scent filling him, he couldn't think too much. Sbe'd shown him more than he'd even imagined. She wasn't cool. Never cool. She'd stunned him, left him throbbing, though not with raw desire. That had been satiated. He ached with an emotion more complicated than simple passion. She would never believe him. She wasn't a woman to rush into anything. Even during the pounding beat of desire, when the intensity had seemed too much, she'd been willing to draw out the moment, prolonging it until he'd thought he would go mad before the final driving force had washed over him. She hadn't been in control any more than he'd been. She'd just enticed him to the point where he'd been reluctant to see it end.

Now he taunted himself in a different way, wanting to spill out his thoughts and feelings to her and knowing that he couldn't. Shifting to lift his weight from her, he kept her close, the length of her flat against him. He couldn't let her go—not yet.

Hours later, Kate opened her eyes to the faint blush of dawn streaming through the venetian blinds and heard the sound of rain, but didn't move. With every breath she absorbed his scent. She hadn't realized until now that she'd missed waking up next to a man, missed the intimacy of a night's lovemaking and of the morning after. As Tony stirred, nuzzling closer, she kissed his chest. "Bran or cornflakes?"

"You." He draped an arm around her and whispered in a husky morning voice, "You're beautiful."

As he pulled her onto him, molding them together, she felt her body swell with a wanting as intense as their first time. And as his mouth's sweetness and warmth covered hers and his fingers skimmed her thigh, the magic began again.

He was tense yet supple; he was grace and muscle. She traced her fingertips along the curves in his upper arms, down his lean ribs, along the sides of his strong thighs. She kissed and tasted, and listened to his pleased moan as her lips enjoyed the saltiness of his flesh. She gave what she'd received. They lay bathed in the glow of dawn's light, the scent of intimacy hanging in the air. A force of more than desire bound them, and more than something as emotionless as sex arched her toward him. With wild, hungry kisses he drove her to the limits of sanity and she listened to the raindrops of an early-morning shower and knew she would never experience another rainy day and not remember the joy of this one.

Minutes later, with a sense of contentment that Kate hadn't believed could exist, she burrowed deeper under the sheet as he eased away from her. She considered lazily closing her eyes again, but within seconds, the rich aroma of coffee drifted toward her. Sighing, she untangled herself from the sheet and rolled over.

Grinning, sitting on the edge of the bed, Tony held a coffee cup beneath her nose. "It stopped raining."

"How did you know I needed coffee?" she asked sleepily, pushing herself to a sitting position, then taking the cup from his hand.

"Dynamos must run on something," he teased.

She brushed her cheek against his, aware that she'd stepped willingly into his embrace, sure that she could separate love and passion. Other people shared one without offering the other, she'd told herself. Now she wondered if any of that was really possible. She'd lost herself in his arms, given everything. She'd done something that she'd vowed never to do again. She'd opened not only her body but also a small place in her heart to this man.

He placed a fingertip upon the space between her brows, making her aware she was frowning. "If I assure you that this relationship will be a neat and orderly one, will you smile?"

Kate sighed again. Did he read minds? she wondered. She sensed the danger—the possibility that love would sneak up on her. She knew better, didn't she? Somehow she had to protect herself. "Can anyone do that?" she asked. Damp from his shower, his dark hair shone with red highlights. Lightly she toyed with a strand of it behind his ear.

"Probably not. But we'll pretend—"

Kate peered at him over the rim of the cup. "Pretend?"

"Yeah, you know the kind of thing you once did as a kid."

"I never did."

He kissed her nose. "Lies make the nose grow. Your mother told me about how you would swipe her heels and dress up like a princess."

Kate sagged toward him in resignation and moaned against his collarbone.

"Your secrets are out," he mumbled, burying his face in her hair. "You're as prone to wild imaginings as the rest of us."

"And you'll never let me hear the end of it, will you?"

"Never."

Kate pressed her lips against the curve of his neck and stayed still for a long moment, yearning for the closeness to continue.

"You're a sleepyhead," he murmured in a slow, lazy manner that made Kate want to stay in bed even longer. "Teresa left some painting clothes here. I think that they'll fit you."

She pushed a hand against his chest and drew back. The eyes staring down at her were filled with laughter. "Why would I need them?"

"Expect a day like you've never known before."

Kate narrowed her eyes. She wasn't quite sure if she should be excited or cautious. "A day like I've never—"

He skimmed the soft roundness of her hip, then backed off the bed and laughed. "Stick with me, kid," he said in a terrible impersonation of Humphrey Bogart.

Minutes later, dressed, Kate stood before the mirror to gather her hair into a rubber band. Before she could secure the ponytail, Tony grabbed her hand in passing. "Come on."

Her hair still flying loose, she trailed out of the bedroom behind him. "Are you going to tell me where we're going today?"

"You're mine for the whole day, aren't you?"

"I can't deny that," she said, laughing softly as he slowed his stride to tug her close.

"I never thought I'd hear it."

She frowned, tilting her head back to see his eyes. "What didn't you expect to hear?"

"You agreeing with me about anything," he teased.

"I'm a reformed woman. Tell me where we're going."

"To pan for gold."

He stepped away, but she balked, fixing her sneakers to the carpet. "We aren't."

"We aren't?" he mimicked, sending her a faked scowl.

Kate stood firm. "That's crazy. You don't actually believe that you'll find—?" Her protest remained incomplete as he kissed the tip of her nose.

"Does it matter? The fun is in the anticipation. And you know about anticipation, don't you?"

Did she ever!

Hours later, with night closing in, Kate's back ached from bending. Her feet were soaked. Her fingernails could have belonged to a coal miner. And her smile seemed plastered on her face. Fun! She'd had fun, she thought in amazement as she stood beneath the shower and closed her eyes, luxuriating in the cool water running down her skin.

In the kitchen she heard Tony whistling a Sousa march. His light spirit was inexhaustible. Contagious. She couldn't recall a day in her life when she'd done something as wasteful as simply enjoying the sunlight, when she'd actually spent minutes just contemplating the colors of rocks.

She was slipping over the edge, she realized minutes later. She entered the kitchen to find him standing by the stove and knew that not a day, a week or a month with him would be enough.

He looked up from the frying pan at the click of her heels on the tiled floor. "Ah, a mermaid."

Laughter bubbled into her throat. "You have an unlimited imagination." The scent of fish frying wafted toward her as she skirted the table to close a cabinet. Kate didn't plan on being nosy, but she'd noticed the disorder inside, and frowning, she began to circle the room, opening and closing cupboards. "This kitchen is—"

Tony knew exactly what was happening behind him. He'd seen her sterile apartment. "Nice, huh?" he said in a voice filled with a mixture of amusement and a good-natured dare not to make a comment.

Kate couldn't resist. She'd noted the subtle differences between them before. She planned her time so as to arrive early. He was easily distracted, arriving on time, but barely. Inwardly she responded to situations with a passionate nature, yet presented a calm facade. He responded openly, sometimes in a light-hearted manner, at others with a quick, passionate energy that caught a person off guard. But he always reacted. Now, looking up from a drawer filled with clothespins, electrical tape and anything else that didn't seem to have a definite home, she saw a more visible difference.

"You would work more efficiently if you put your cooking utensils in the drawer next to the stove," she said in her best impersonation of the pedantic Edgar Svenson. "If everything has a proper place..."

Tony turned a thunderous glare upon her that was more comical than threatening, and Kate laughed, raising her hands in surrender. "All right. I give up." Smiling, she glanced down at the drawer again and retrieved a golf ball. "What else don't I know about you?" she asked curiously, dropping the ball into the drawer and closing it. "Are you a superb athlete?"

"Superb." He puffed his chest and flexed a biceps. "I swing a mean croquet mallet."

Kate stifled a giggle. "And baseball bat?" she asked, arching a brow.

"That and all that other stuff," he said offhand-edly. "Jock-on-the-campus type."

Life was a playground, she reflected.

"And you?"

"I trudge to exercise class four mornings a week before I'm awake enough to know that I'm there." She shrugged her shoulders, imitating the stance of the guilty. "At least I used to."

"Don't worry." He playfully caressed her backside in passing. "You're not getting out of shape. There's been plenty of exercise."

Kate nodded agreeably and joined him at the table. "I've been using that as an excuse, too. I read somewhere that sex burns up two hundred calories." She watched a look of incredulity settle upon his face. Masking her delight, she maintained a serious expression. "I reasoned that was as good a reason as any for enjoying myself."

"Did you?"

"Oh, that I did," she assured him, and finally gave in to a laugh.

"We both did," he murmured softly against her throat.

She was nearly late Monday morning. Miss Punctuality, she mused self-deprecatingly, arriving one minute before her workday began.

Rushing into the bank, her umbrella dripping a trail of water through the employees' entrance to the lounge, she was dismayed by the thought that Tony's life-style might be rubbing off on her.

Joanna opened the door that led in to the tellers' section, looked back at the sound of Kate's hurried approach and arched a brow. "Busy weekend?"

Kate felt her face grow warm. "Is the bank robbery still getting space in the newspaper?" she asked, noting the morning edition in Joanna's hand.

"The hero, too." In the manner of someone taking part in some long-distance relay, she handed the rolled newspaper to Kate and preceded her into the large room.

Strolling toward her office, Kate scanned the story about the bank robbery. Prominently mentioned was Tony Patelli. Kate hoped that his involvement would help him with Mr. Svenson.

Some wishes came true, it seemed. The left side of Edgar Svenson's face twitched upward in a sign of greeting. "Good morning, Ms. Elliot," he said as he entered her office. He stopped before her desk and ceremoniously set down a manila file folder to the left of the newspaper. "Did you read the story?"

"I only glanced at it."

"We were very fortunate. It could have been a difficult day for Westcot Bank. Investors like to know their money is safe. Yes, yes, fortunate we were."

"Thanks to Mr. Patelli," Kate said quickly.

"Indeed." He nodded in agreement, a rarity for him.

"I assume that it would be good for the bank's image to issue a loan to the man who foiled a bank robbery."

"Oh, yes, that's true, too. But emotional responses don't belong in a bank." Hands clasped behind his back, he rocked on his heels and stared down at her. "Remember that. We deal in facts. And the facts are very good about Mr. Patelli." He motioned toward the manila folder. "His financial holdings are excellent."

"Excellent?" Kate murmured, and bent her head to flip open the folder. Excellent was a mild description. Anthony John Patelli had a bank account, a trust fund and stock ownership that would make anyone drool; the bottom line was staggering. Kate didn't understand anything at that moment. If Tony had this kind of money, then why was he requesting a loan?

Tony listened to the rain pelting at the window while he finished dressing for his appointment at the bank. Barring a hitch, he'd be early. That would please Kate. Properly dressed in navy sport coat and gray slacks, he guessed, except for needing a haircut, that he was ready for the scrutinizing Svenson.

Slipping his wallet into his back pocket, he strolled toward the bed to throw it together. The scent of Kate's perfume drifted toward him as if she'd staked a claim there. Instant pleasure surged through him. At that moment he should have been a happy man, but he had a problem.

She'd made love with him, but he'd sensed her reluctance to let her emotions take her beyond passion. She'd given him her body, but he knew that winning her heart wouldn't be easy.

She would always be self-sufficient and independent. He had no problem with that. He was used to women who made their own decisions. His sister Teresa had always had a mind of her own until Jon's domination had become overbearing. And Michelle had been a spitfire, firm and strong in her beliefs. But those two women had both understood something that Kate chose to ignore. Love meant emotional sharing, a support system that stole nothing from the other person. To accept that, Kate had to trust him. He wasn't sure how to succeed in making her do that. Somehow he would have to convince her that he wasn't like that other man who'd breezed in and out of her life. He planned to stay.

Watch in hand, Tony slipped it on while striding toward the door. As he reached for the doorknob, the phone rang. He hesitated, then wheeled around. He should let it ring, he told himself, but he was one of those people who would literally jump over furniture to answer a ringing telephone.

He snatched up the receiver on the second ring and offered a greeting.

"Tony."

The familiar voice sounded weaker than usual and strained. "Teresa?"

"Tony, I..." Her voice trembled audibly. "Oh, Tony..."

"What's wrong? Sara?"

"No," she said quickly, her voice catching. "Sara is fine."

He let a breath of relief slip out, but couldn't ignore the tears that he heard in his sister's voice. He cradled the phone in his hand. "What's wrong then?"

She was clearly struggling for words. "I need you," she said, sobbing as she spoke.

* * *

Not for the first time, Kate glared at the clock in the employees' lounge. She'd expected Tony to stroll into the bank at least fifteen minutes early. When the clock had shown that only five minutes were left, she'd grabbed a candy from her pack of Tootsie Rolls, paced her office, then had gone to the vending machine.

While a disposable cup filled with coffee, Kate pushed back the sleeve of her suit jacket and glanced again at her wristwatch. Where was he? He had two minutes to get there. Only two, then he'd be late.

As nervousness made her stomach do a flip-flop, she dumped the cup and rushed back to her office with hurried steps, hoping to see Tony lounging in a chair. He wasn't. Instead, as she rounded the desk, she saw a message had been taken while she'd been gone.

Dropping onto her chair, she stared at the note. He'd canceled the appointment. After all she'd gone through, including groveling before Svenson, Tony had canceled the appointment. She read the message three times, as if it were difficult to comprehend. *Something important happened. Call you.* What could be more important? she thought, suddenly so annoyed that she balled the note and tossed it into the wastebasket with such fury that it ricocheted off the side of the basket and fell to the floor.

She breathed hard, trying to calm herself. He wouldn't miss the appointment unless he'd had good reason. He wouldn't, she repeated several times, and hoped she wasn't fooling herself.

* * *

Stuck in a line of traffic, Tony peered between the swishing windshield wipers. Impatient, he cursed the long waits at the red lights, the driver who cut him off, the train with its fifty-two cars, which he counted as if he were ten years old again.

When he finally stood before Teresa's door, he leaned upon the doorbell. If she didn't answer right away, he planned to use his key. But Teresa flung open the door on the first chime. She offered no pretense that she hadn't been crying. Her red-rimmed eyes met his for a second, then closed. "I feel like such a fool," she said, and fell into his arms.

He stroked her hair and held her, saying nothing. During the drive to her house, he'd guessed what was wrong. Hell, he'd sensed trouble months ago.

She stepped away, sniffing to hold back the tears. "You know, don't you?"

He kept a hand on her waist, not wanting her to draw away. "Why don't you tell me?"

"Telling you isn't the problem," she said, no longer able to suppress her tears. Sighing in disgust, she yanked a tissue from her jeans pocket, dabbed quickly at her eyes and blew her nose, then shoved the tissue back into her pocket. Seeming to brace herself for the inevitable, she spoke in a tight voice. "Telling you is easy. But how do I tell Papa that I'm getting a divorce?"

* * *

By the time the bank closed, the rain had dwindled to a drizzle. Kate rushed to her car. Avoiding puddles, she tried to ignore her doubts and suspicions. Was Tony losing interest in the amusement park? Had he only wanted the business as long as it was out of his reach, when success or failure hadn't mattered?

She'd honestly begun to believe that Tony was dependable. If she couldn't rely on him to keep an appointment, did she really believe he'd stick around for her, be near when she needed him?

She swore softly, annoyed at her own gullibility. Wanting to calm down, she drove to her mother's gallery, hoping to relax before seeing Tony again.

The moment she walked in, her mother pounced upon her. "Oh, I'm so glad you came!" Claire was dressed in something that resembled a Gypsy's garb. Kate didn't need to see the label to know it was a designer original. Looking away from the brilliant lavender and red outfit, she scanned the room. Several pastel paintings adorned one white wall in a far corner, and an abstract took center stage in an alcove. "You've acquired a few new paintings."

"More than a few."

Kate meandered toward the photograph that her mother had been framing.

"And one of them is missing."

Frowning, Kate whirled around, hoping that she'd misunderstood. Immediately she knew that she hadn't. Her mother was pale. "Missing? What do you mean, missing?'' she asked, even as her attention strayed to the man lounging carelessly in the storeroom doorway. She swung her eyes away from Jimmy and spoke to her mother in a low voice. "Missing or stolen?"

As if concerned that he might have heard, her mother painted a smile upon her face and turned toward him. "You may leave now, Jimmy. I don't have any more work for you today."

Maintaining his indolent stance, he pushed away from the doorjamb, his dark eyes narrowing upon Kate before he nodded his head at her mother.

Claire waited until the door closed behind him. "Katie, really," she reprimanded.

"You don't think he would steal it?" Kate asked with incredulity.

"Don't be silly. I'm sure it isn't stolen." Her eyes darted around the room, a trace of hysteria seeming only a breath away. "It's just misplaced," she insisted more sharply. Her hand gripping Kate's wrist, she tugged her along toward the storeroom. "Help me look for it. With so many crates—well, you know I'm not the most organized person."

Kate couldn't suppress a chiding tone. "I warned you not to hire him."

Her mother skirted a crate. "How can my daughter be such a cynic? Kate, you can't jump to conclusions and make such an accusation."

Kate rolled her eyes. "It's conducive to banker's pallor," she said by way of excuse.

Her mother sent her a semblance of a smile before directing her attention toward a shelf of paintings.

Kate noted by the frame and photograph on a small table that her mother had obviously been working there when she realized her problem. Turning away from the table, Kate crouched before a crate to begin a search of her own. "Whose was it?"

As if too preoccupied to have registered what she'd said, Claire cast a puzzled stare at Kate over her shoulder.

"Whose painting?" Kate repeated.

"Oh, a very nasty, temperamental man."

Kate eyed an unopened crate. "Then why do you accept his work?"

"Because he's a genius."

Her mother's broad-minded attitude about some people's hefty faults always amazed Kate. "Mother, have you opened this crate yet?" Kate motioned toward it while visually hunting for a tool to pry it open.

"If I misplaced it, Kate, I must have seen it. How could it be in there?"

Kate rose from her bent position to scan several paintings ready for framing that were resting on a lower shelf. "Did you see it?"

"Well—yes." Hesitancy colored her mother's voice. Standing, she met Kate's eyes squarely. "No, I really didn't. Jimmy was supposed to check off the paintings on a list as he unpacked them. And..." She stretched for a clipboard on her desk. "And you see..." She tapped a finger at a name on the list. "He checked off that it had been unpacked."

Kate didn't wait for her to finish speaking. Crowbar in hand, she pried one side off the crate. Several paintings, many framed, were neatly packed in a mesh screen. Kate removed them one by one, discarding the heavy corrugated cardboard between them, then setting them aside. "Mother, he doesn't know art. He could have done that to make it look as if he'd been working hard when he hadn't been."

"Oh, Kate, now why would he—?"

Kate realized her efforts were futile. The missing painting wasn't in the crate. "Because people can't always be depended on to do what they promise," she insisted all too knowingly. "Where are the rest of your local Picassos?"

"Over here." Her mother hustled toward a table at the back of the storeroom. "Jimmy looked through these...."

"Why don't you look through them?" Kate suggested with measurable slowness, hoping to quell her exasperation. "Please."

Sighing heavily and frowning, her mother acquiesced. "Katie, you have to learn to trust some people to do..."

Her voice faded, and Kate guessed why. "You found it, right?"

"Oh, yes." Her mother pivoted, smiling. "That's a relief," she said breezily, as if she hadn't spent any time at all worrying and searching.

"I really wish you would get someone else to help you here," Kate insisted.

Claire patted her hand in passing. "Kate, he made one mistake. That's no reason to let him go."

"He's made a lot of mistakes," Kate said, uttering a ragged sigh, doubting she was making a dent in her mother's steely stubbornness.

"That was before." Her mother held up the painting before her and tilted her head, first one way, then the other, in an admiring fashion. "The man really is quite brilliant." A tiny frown etched a line between her brows. "If only he was more pleasant," she said almost wistfully.

Kate pursed her lips to stop herself from saying more. Life just wasn't as peachy keen as her mother wanted to believe.

Claire's heavy sigh jarred Kate from private thoughts, and she saw her mother's eyes zeroing in on her in a manner that reminded her of her youth. "Why do you still look troubled?"

Kate wagged her head. "It's nothing."

Before Kate could step away, her mother grabbed her arm.

"I'm not upset," she replied, attempting a denial despite her mother's knowing stare. Breathing hard, Kate moved to one side. "Tony didn't show for the appointment that I made for him with Mr. Svenson. I should have known better." She paced in a circle around the worktable and the crates. "If he was a different kind of man..."

"Did he call?"

Kate paused. "He left a message about something important coming up."

Her mother arched a brow. "Why aren't you giving him a chance?"

Kate whirled around to face her squarely. "How many dreamers do I need drifting in and out of my life before I learn a lesson?"

Sadness clouded her mother's eyes.

Kate didn't want to see it, but she couldn't stop the doubts. She was amazed that her mother could look away and ignore the obvious.

"I don't know what lesson you think you need to learn. But you're jumping to conclusions, and I wonder why."

"Because nothing is clear," Kate retorted. "I learned that he didn't need to show. He didn't really need the loan. Did you know that?"

Her mother smiled, making Kate aware that she was more perplexed than angry.

"His father owns a few small, intimate Italian restaurants," Kate went on, calmer now. "He owns a run-down amusement park, drives a beat-up truck..." She paused as she remembered the Porsche. "He gives the impression that he's scrimping for pennies and he's loaded."

As her mother's hand touched her shoulder, Kate saw her eyes gleam with delight. "Well, that's a rather nice surprise, isn't it?"

Suddenly thoughtful, Kate stared at her, taken aback by her mother's optimistic response. "Yes, it is," she was forced to admit. "But it's also puzzling."

Chapter Nine

Typical of an Arizona summer day, the rain stopped as abruptly as it had begun. Kate sidestepped several puddles on the way from her car to the amusement park. Head bent, she concentrated on the ground. Mud oozed up around the soles of her pumps. Dumb move, she thought, wishing she'd changed into sneakers.

She reached gravel, scraped her soles on it, then at the clang of a wrench, pivoted toward the merry-go-round.

His back to her, Tony was squatting, partially hidden by the giant horse and dusk's shadows. As if keyed in to some private radar, he braced himself on his heels and turned his head. "Hey?" Smiling, he dropped the wrench and rose in one swift move.

Stopping only a few feet from the platform, Kate remained motionless, patiently waiting. "You didn't come."

If he caught a hint of her mood, it didn't seem to faze him. Bending, he yanked a rag from the back pocket of his jeans and rubbed at a smudge on his palm. "You got the message, didn't you?"

"Yes," she said stiffly. "'Something important came up.'" She couldn't keep anger from her tone. "What?" Tense, she curled her fingers over the top of her shoulder bag. "What could be more important?"

Tony took a deep breath. He realized that her trust was in jeopardy but didn't know why. "My sister needed me. By the time I was free, I knew the bank was closed. What would have been the point?"

As his dark gaze locked with hers, Kate acknowledged that she'd been imagining a wealth of excuses. And he'd presented her with the one, the only one she hadn't expected. She understood such a binding force. Nothing would stand in her way if her mother needed her.

She twisted her head, averting her eyes for a second, the foolishness of her own quick anger haunting her. How dumb could she be? she asked herself, embarrassed. Why hadn't she given him a chance to explain before letting her anger rise? And if she didn't want to fall in love with him, if she felt nothing for him, then why did he matter to her so much? Why had doubts about him been only a breath away?

"I'm sorry if I caused you a problem, Kate."

As she swung back to face him, Tony tossed the rag aside. Kate saw the troubled frown marring his brow. "You said your sister needed you. Is something wrong?"

"It's not good. Divorce."

"Oh, Tony." Kate recalled the horrible days before and after her own divorce. Failure was never easy to accept.

"About the appointment, Kate—"

She shook her head. "I understand." She met his eyes. Remembering his father's views about marriage, she knew his family might face some rocky moments in the days to come. "Something more important did happen."

He watched the play of emotions cross her face and heard the hint of sympathy in her voice. Her understanding enveloped him. Could a man's knees weaken at a few words? he wondered. "But was there a problem?"

She smiled wanly. "No. Mr. Svenson was quite amiable, since he'd already seen your financial report. He probably wonders though why you asked for the loan. So do I," she admitted.

Tony caught the slight change in her tone and read puzzlement in her eyes. "I don't want to touch that money," he said simply.

He saw a frown pinch her brows. "Tony, that doesn't make sense. For that matter, none of this does," she said with a sweep of her arm.

"Don't scowl," he teased, mimicking her glowering look in an attempt to lighten her mood.

Kate hedged for a second, then asked bluntly, "Why are you playing around with this?"

"It's not my style to tinker with yachts."

Confused, she stared up at him as he lounged against one of the painted horses. She lived half of her waking hours surrounded by money, by people trying to get more. He had more than enough and was snubbing his nose at it. But then he was a fighter—a spirited, tenacious man who had chosen a business challenge to save himself, to have something tangible to fight for, and expel the anger that had been mingled with his grief.

As he wrapped one hand firmly around the pole and leaned toward her, offering her his other hand, she stared at the broad, callused palm. Her heart opened to him. She'd seen his gentle side, she'd sensed how much he cared for his family. Desperately she struggled to cast away her doubts. Her mother was right. She wasn't giving him a chance—or herself. Sometimes it was best not to think too much. Feel. Just feel. Forget everything else, she thought, stepping forward and placing her hand in his.

He pulled her up in a sweeping movement to join him on the platform. "You came to give me hell, didn't you?" He didn't wait for an answer but caught her to him, holding her close, so close that she had to tilt back her head to meet his eyes.

"I don't know what to say."

Every moment was a challenge for them, Tony realized, twisting away to flick a switch. He sensed the shield she wanted to erect around her heart, the one that kept her from him. Yet she was too strong a woman to let one man scar her so deeply. Not for the first time, he wondered what part of her past he was really battling. "A smile would do," he assured her, gathering her into his arms again.

Her head fell back and her lips curved. Lights suddenly glittered above her like a hundred Fourth of July sparklers, and the soft, swaying beat of a waltz wafted through the air as the whirling motion of the ride began.

"I told you there's a white horse for a princess," he murmured against her jaw.

As he lifted her onto a horse, Kate gave in to a pleased laugh. "I haven't been on a merry-go-round in years."

"Then it was time."

Kate felt the hard beat of his heart against her breast. A peacefulness surrounded her, but as he whispered endearments against her ear and his voice caressed her, he brewed a storm within her to rival the one that had raged earlier in the day. Want blended with need. She twisted to face him, coiling her arms around his neck. In his lips she tasted both promise and demand, a wild insistence that she suddenly craved. He wanted her. At this time, that was enough.

One day turned into two and then into a week, and Kate found herself slipping into a routine she'd never expected.

Sitting in the employees' lounge at the bank, she cradled a coffee cup in her hands and squinted against the hazy sunlight streaming through the blinds. Her thoughts were consumed with deciding what to wear to a birthday party for Tony's cousin Carlo. Inwardly she was a little nervous about meeting the whole clan.

"I truly hate Mondays," Joanna moaned seconds later, plopping onto the closest sofa and cutting into Kate's thoughts. "I wish that I knew your secret."

Kate tipped her head. "Secret?"

"For coming to work and looking as if there's nowhere else you'd rather be."

Kate winked. "I'm a good actress."

Joanna drew back and eyed Kate as if she were an alien. "You? Ms. Westcot Bank? You'd rather be somewhere else?"

"Was I that bad?"

"Not bad." Joanna muffled a yawn. "Conscientious." Sipping her coffee, she peered at Kate over the rim of her cup for a long moment.

"How was exercise class this morning?" Kate asked.

"I missed it."

Kate noted that Joanna didn't look too guilty. "The biceps man?"

"The attorney."

Kate concentrated on her friend. "It's on again?"

Joanna's lips spread wide in a pleased smile. "What can I say? He expounds about torts and dispositions and my heart pitter-patters," she said and laughed as she placed a hand to her chest.

Kate smiled. "That's great."

"I think so." Joanna suddenly perked up, her back straightening. "I've been thinking. There can be only one reason for such a drastic change in you."

Kate wasn't sure she wanted to hear the rest of what Joanna planned to say.

"Love," she proclaimed.

Love, Kate grinned, feeling fifteen again.

Joanna set down her cup, her eyes growing round. "You are, aren't you?" Though Kate said nothing, Joanna beamed. "Well, good for you."

Kate responded with what she knew must be a feeble smile. Though she didn't want to entertain niggling doubts about Tony and herself, another man had taught her a lesson three years ago. She knew that she didn't want to lose control of her life, didn't want to let emotions long buried resurface and make her believe in promises again. She could still remember too vividly how vulnerable, how defenseless she'd once been and didn't want any of that. But oh, to love again, to believe in love again! Kate couldn't deny she longed to do just that.

Because of a late-afternoon appointment, she got home barely in time to peel off her suit and slip on a peach-colored summer dress before Tony arrived.

At seven o'clock, she and Tony entered his father's home to find rooms overflowing with people, children chasing about, and voices raised in glee and conversation. The Patelli clan was noisy. Laughter mingled with affectionate arguments, and the aroma of a rich tomato sauce permeated the air.

Seated between Tony and his father in the family dining room, Kate lifted her wineglass to find it full again. As the noise level rose to a deafening buzz, she dared to start a conversation with Tony. "Is it always like this?" she asked, speaking at least a decibel louder than usual.

"Always." He leaned close, bending his head so she could talk normally. "Overwhelming, aren't they?"

Kate couldn't disagree. "Immensely."

Tony offered an understanding grin, then kissed the shell of her ear. He'd never felt so unsure about a woman in his whole life. But then Kate wasn't just any woman.

He liked the look of her here, he decided. With her blond hair and fair skin she looked pale in comparison to the Patelli crew. Though she'd been quiet, she'd also laughed freely, something that brought him pleasure. He'd noted the swiftness of her smile whenever his father had talked to her. Best of all, he'd seen the softness of her gentle soul emerging as she'd held Roberto's newborn in her arms. It was a sight that had simultaneously stabbed Tony with anguish and swept pleasure through him. At that moment he'd wanted to have her forever.

Pleasurably he fingered a strand of her silky hair as she turned away to answer his father's question. He still wanted to touch her—to kiss her. Right now.

Something made him hold back. Though he wanted to think of being always with her, he couldn't imagine any moments beyond this one.

Kate answered Luigi's question with a smile, then swung a look back at Tony. In this room full of bright spirits she couldn't fathom the reason for his sudden frown.

"Tony?" Luigi sat forward, cocking his head to see his son. "Have you thought about what we discussed?"

Kate would have had to be blind not to see the tensing in Tony's jaw.

Picking up his wineglass, he shook his head. "No."

Sighing heavily, his father dropped his napkin onto his plate and shoved it away. "When?"

"Pop, I don't know." She saw him meet his father's eyes, heard annoyance tinge his speech. "Just not now, okay?"

Kate waited until his father looked away. "What was that about?" She'd slept with the man seated beside her, she reasoned. She had a right to be nosy.

His smile didn't reach his eyes. "He needs help at one of his restaurants."

She might have believed his answer if he hadn't avoided her eyes.

"Patience isn't one of his great traits."

Kate forced a smile to answer his. Nothing was wrong, she told herself. She was imagining everything. As Tony became an unwilling audience to an uncle's tirade about the city's football team, Kate gathered plates, then carried them into the kitchen.

When she returned to the living room, Tony's nephew was playing the accordion. Two of his aunts broke into laughter in the middle of their debate about a recipe. Only one person seemed out of place in this large, close-knit family. Noting his scowl, Kate had avoided Teresa's husband for most of the evening.

As family members crowded around the table for their slice of birthday cake, Kate circled the room and eyed the multitude of photographs adorning the walls and mantel. Stepping away from an old family photograph of Luigi as a boy, she searched the sea of faces for Tony. Trapped by his Aunt Rosa, a robust woman whose hands constantly moved, he kept smiling and nodding at whatever she was saying, but Kate registered the worry in his eyes.

"Are you going to become a member of this big, happy family?"

Kate swung around in response to the question. Still not smiling, Teresa's husband scanned the room, a trace of disgust creeping into his voice. "They're always all smiles."

Unlike Jon, Kate had thought the happiness around her was wonderful. She narrowed her eyes and stared at his profile for a long moment. He was an elegant-looking man, but wore a disdainful sneer, sipping his wine and making a face as if its flavor offended his senses. He seemed miserably dissatisfied—with everything.

In a confiding manner, he leaned closer, propping a hand against the wall near her shoulder. "Because if you are, you'd better be warned."

Kate locked her gaze with his. "Warned?"

"It's not so great."

Kate looked past him for some excuse to escape the bitterness that she heard in his voice.

"We aren't making it work. Teresa and I. You see that, don't you?"

Kate didn't know what to say. The problems in his marriage weren't her business. She didn't know this man well enough for him to be telling her something so personal.

"Well, none of them do," he said with a sweep of his arm. "They don't want to. But then that's the Patelli way. They're quite a group—all of them. They keep avoiding what's obvious. Teresa, too. Our marriage is over and she refused to really face it. It doesn't coincide with some grand illusion she has about marriage."

Kate shifted her stance, wishing for some way to step away. She knew Teresa had said something to Tony about a divorce, but from what Jon was saying,

Tony's sister hadn't yet totally given up on her marriage.

"Well, I have ideas about what a marriage should be, too." He snorted. "But when I need her, is she around? Hell, no."

Fearful, Kate met his eyes again.

"She isn't," he insisted, sounding annoyed, as if Kate's silence meant that she doubted his words.

In a way she did. She couldn't find fault with Teresa for being a caring mother and placing Sara's best interests first.

"What a farce! What a damn farce," he muttered before turning away.

Kate watched him weave slightly as he wound his way to the makeshift bar to pour himself another drink. He seemed to have had too many already, she thought sadly.

Slipping back into the shadows, Kate couldn't escape disturbing thoughts. Across the room, Teresa was clearly forcing smiles for the family's sake. Kate wondered if she really was the only one to see the other woman's unhappiness. Were the Patellis so caught up in some idealistic image of the perfect couple that they couldn't tell how miserable two of their own were? Did they believe that if problems were ignored, they'd go away? Life just wasn't so simple.

"Such a wonderful couple," a voice said, jarring Kate from her thoughts.

Aunt Rosa stood before her, beaming, waving her hands as if leading an orchestra and finally letting them settle upon Kate's cheeks for an affectionate squeeze. "Our Tony is a smart boy."

Kate managed a nod.

"And you're a smart girl, heh? Ah, such a wonderful thing love is."

Love? Kate asked herself, frowning as the older woman plodded away. Throughout the evening, one relative or another had taken her aside. The approach was always different. A wink, a coy smile, a speculative comment. The question—never bluntly spoken but nonetheless implied—had always been the same, had always alluded to a commitment, an engagement, a marriage between Tony and herself.

Despite the intimacy she and Tony had shared, he had never once said that he loved her, and she had told herself that she never expected him to. Why then did she almost wish she *had* heard those exact words from him?

"Want to leave?"

Facing Tony, she curled an arm around his waist. Why was she even looking for change between them? Fiercely she clung to the pleasure she'd heard in his voice. "Your place or mine?"

"Mine." Tony chuckled. "It's closer."

His lips muffled her words of agreement. In his arms she realized that she could almost forget the danger of promises.

Sunlight warmed the room as the alarm clock wound down to a faint sound like the droning of a pesky mosquito in Kate's ears. Eyes squeezed tight, she groped along the edge of the nightstand for the clock.

Beside her, groggy from sleep, Tony groaned. "I hate that thing."

She glanced at the clock and moved back under the covers. So did his hand. As it coursed its way downward and his fingers fluttered across her thigh, Kate giggled and curled toward him, anticipating fireworks. "Are you even awake?"

"I'm awake." He scooted down, letting his mouth linger between her breasts.

She whispered his name, feeling the inevitable shiver slithering over her as he drew the nipple into his mouth. "You have a definite knack—" Kate sighed softly "—for making me forget everything. Even time," she murmured and shuddered in response to the stroking of his tongue, the fingers skimming the inside of her thigh.

"Plenty of time." He managed to utter the words, then groaned.

Like a butterfly's caress, his mouth grazed the softness of her belly, the firmness of her thighs. Kate closed her eyes, all thoughts tumbling from her mind. Gasping softly, she arched her back as his touch began to overshadow everything else. In less time than it took to draw breath, she rode a wave of sensation. Desire had never been like this before.

He made her forget everything but him. As if she had no will of her own, she followed the command of his hands. Limbs suddenly felt too heavy to lift. She'd drunk nothing, yet felt the light-headedness of intoxication.

Wherever he touched, wherever his tongue stroked, her flesh tingled. Longing made her tremble. She clung, urging his mouth to taste, arching against him in a gesture of welcome, of invitation. She was a creature of her senses, caught up in the soft kisses, the gentle caresses, the murmured words.

They taunted each other even as they pleasured. And all the time they were traveling the same path. As he shifted, his mouth hungrily at her breast again, Kate caught her breath and stretched to take in air. She moaned, aching mindlessly, and dug her hands into his shoulders to pull him even closer, not believing the need that was driving her to blend with this man.

Beneath her hands his muscles rippled, and as his fingers glided over her, she wrapped her legs around his buttocks. She drew him even closer until his body fused with hers, until he filled her.

She met the dark eyes staring down at her, and as he drove deeply, she moved against and with him, wondering if it were possible to die of wanting for one man.

Breathing raggedly, shuddering, feeling him tremble, knowing they were slipping away, all she could think about was traveling with him again.

For long moments afterward, Tony stared at the sunlight streaking into the room. She'd sent him over the edge. He listened to her breathing, more evenly now, and curled her closer to him. She'd driven him. He'd heard her sighs of pleasure, her moans, and he'd dived over the brink of sanity, feeling a fierceness that had seemed foreign to him taking command. He'd felt the trembling arousal from his adolescence sweep through him during those moments.

Tugging her tightly to him, he felt the tip of a nipple against his chest, the warm moistness of her on his thigh. There was no peace to quell his aching. It went beyond desire, beyond the flame of passion. He plunged one hand into the thick mass of her hair and pressed his mouth hard against hers yet again. He wanted to keep her close, to keep a part of himself in her, to know that she was his, that she couldn't escape. But if he wanted all these things and more, why did he hesitate? Why wasn't he saying the words that would tell her what she really meant to him?

Chapter Ten

At four o'clock the next day, Kate punched at the numbers on the telephone, then waited impatiently for Tony to answer. "You got it," she said before he could offer a hello.

"Thank you."

Kate giggled. "Stop it. I meant the loan. You got the loan."

"Hey, that's great!"

She heard the pleasure in his voice and couldn't stop smiling. "We need to celebrate, but I have to go to my mother's gallery first. I promised her days ago that I'd drop off a lithograph I'd found by some obscure artist. Meet me there. We'll have dinner and then—"

"Tell me more about the 'and then' part," he teased.

"And then we'll really celebrate," she promised.

At five minutes to five, Tony wheeled his car around the final corner, heading for the gallery. Squinting against the glare of the setting sun, he slowed the car as he neared his family's restaurant and saw his father strolling out. Raising his gray head and narrowing his eyes, he stopped abruptly on the curb.

Uttering a soft oath, Tony knew he had no choice but to pull up. He braked, aware that he had to make a decision. Uncharacteristically he'd been evading it. The thought of going to California, of leaving Kate, weighed heavily against helping his father with his new restaurant. And he felt the onerous hand of guilt on his shoulder for not being totally honest with her. As he rolled down the window, the smothering heat of summer blasted at him, and he still hadn't found an answer to his dilemma.

"This will only take a moment," his father announced, angling his head as he bent forward to rest a forearm on the open window and peer in at Tony. "I drove out to the park yesterday. It's looking good. Maybe good enough to leave it for a while."

"Pop, look..." Tony started, raising a hand and brushing knuckles at the sweat on his face.

His father arched a brow. "You could escape this heat. You know how."

Tony gave the answer he knew his father wanted to hear. "Yeah, I know how. Go to California."

His father reached in and patted his cheek. "Smart boy I raised."

At the moment Tony didn't fully agree with him.

It was five minutes after five when Kate arrived at the gallery. With one step inside, she felt uneasy. She'd expected to hear her mother's greeting, the sound of footsteps—something. It was surprisingly quiet, too quiet.

"Mother," she called as she ambled through to the exhibition room. Again she felt an icy shiver spiral up her spine, the kind she'd always felt when she was alone at night and heard a strange noise. But it wasn't night, and she wasn't vulnerable to some intruder. So why did she have the same foreboding sensation? And where was her mother? she wondered, annoyed. Kate had assumed that she'd find her bent over her worktable, so engrossed in her task that she wouldn't have heard the buzzer or her daughter's voice.

Rushing her steps now, Kate wound her way around the crates to reach the darkroom where Claire developed photographs. Even before Kate flung open the door and stepped inside, she couldn't believe that her mother would leave the gallery abandoned.

The room, a single bulb hanging from the ceiling and equipped with one counter that held several pans for chemicals, was empty. Where was she? she wondered again. Suddenly frantic, she swung around. The sound of footsteps echoed on the tiled floor of one of the rooms. *Finally.* She released a breath of relief, but the smile on her lips died instantly.

In less time than it took to breathe in again, her throat tightened, and the icy sensation of fear coursed through her veins. "Where's my mother?" she asked the man blocking the doorway.

Slowly Jimmy shook his head. Like a cat eyeing a mouse, he baited her, stalling before answering. "She's not here."

Though he stood in shadow, she could see his eyes. The threat was there as he slowly trailed a path down her body with his squinty eyes.

Kate eyed the distance to the door. She had little choice. With more bravado than bravery, she brushed past him at a quick pace, but didn't manage another step. His hand clamped over her wrist, jolting her to a stop and slamming her so hard against the wall that darkness nearly closed around her.

A scream resounded on the air. The voice didn't sound like her own. It was odd to have a rational thought at such a moment, but more than one fluttered through her mind. No one would hear her. No one was near.

He uttered a sound—a laugh, she realized. "I know what you want."

She felt the sharp cutting edge of the doorjamb in the small of her back, a rough hand groping beneath her skirt. A wave of nausea swept through her. Knee to groin, she reminded herself, but even as she tried to defend herself, he pinned her harder against the wall, blocking her movement.

Seconds ticked by, or were they years? she wondered, struggling blindly, her nails seeking flesh. With some satisfaction she heard him hiss in pain, his breath hot upon her face. Then his mouth closed over hers with a grinding violence. Kate fought on, nearly gagging, almost overwhelmed by the pungency of the garlic on his breath. She knew she had one chance, just one. She relaxed, enduring the hands pawing at her, the tongue invading her mouth. One chance, she thought, and bit down hard.

She'd caught him by surprise. Yelping, he drew back, and in that one precious second she shoved past. Throat dry, heart pounding, she leaped frantically toward the table, lunging for the hammer she'd seen there. Grasping it, she whipped around, raising its claw toward him.

He stumbled forward, holding a shaky hand to the trickle of blood at the corner of his mouth. "Bitch. You think this is the end of it?" he bellowed, but stopped, eyeing her through narrowed slits, as if trying to decide whether she would use the hammer.

Would she? Trembling, she wasn't sure if she would have the backbone to swing it. Still terrified, she gauged the distance to the gallery. She couldn't beat him to the door, couldn't get away.

The thought was snatched from her with the sound of the buzzer, of the gallery door opening. Their eyes locked, fear suddenly springing into his. Kate moved quickly, running toward the front entrance. A lone woman stood there. She swung a look at Kate and her eyes widened.

Clutching at her blouse to close it, Kate wanted to yell at the woman, but no words came out. She heard Jimmy's retreating footsteps at the back of the building but didn't move. Legs trembling beneath her, she swayed back against the counter and grabbed hold of its edge to save herself from slipping to the floor. Her heart thundered, threatening to burst through her chest. She heard a humming in her brain that began to grow so loud that she thought she would pass out. Then in the distance she heard a voice, a soft voice that kept repeating the same words. "What happened? Are you all right?"

She squeezed her eyes shut and drew a deep breath, then another; she didn't want to faint. Was she all right? she wondered as she heard the buzzer on the door again. Blinking, she fought back tears. Instead of a woman, a man stood before her, only the shape of his face clear to her for a brief second.

"Kate."

"Tony." She sagged against him.

"What—what the hell happened?"

Tears flowed. She couldn't stop them. "Jimmy," she managed to say, then shuddered again.

A vile curse slipped from Tony's lips. "He...?" The question stuck in his throat.

Kate shook her head. "No. P-pawed," she stammered, sobbing now. "He just pawed at me."

As she trembled, he tightened his embrace. He rocked and soothed her, letting her weep. He muttered to himself more than once between murmuring unintelligibly to her and stroking her hair, needing her softness to control the hard demand of the anger that filled him. She was safe, he tried to remind himself, but realized he was holding her so tightly that he wondered if she was able to breathe. Anger, coupled with rage, made him tremble, too. He felt her shudder again in his arms and ached. Still offering useless words of comfort to her—to himself—he moved her to a chair.

He stepped back, but her hand clawed at his arm to keep him near. Tony held her again. He grappled for common sense to quiet his own fury, to keep a level head, saw her confusion as he spoke of calling the police.

Kate drew a long, shaky breath, finally raising her eyes not to him but in response to the sound of the door buzzer.

"Katherine." She saw her mother's eyes sweep over her, widening.

"Jimmy," Kate told her, knowing that the condition of her clothes would tell the rest of the story.

"Oh, Katie!"

As imagined horrors clouded her mother's eyes, a tightness swelled in Kate's chest that promised more tears. She swallowed hard, clinging to her mother. "I'm all right now," she insisted. It was a lie, but she felt Claire tremble and searched for a way to quiet her.

"I was frightened. It was so unexpected. But he didn't do any real harm. He scared me. That's all."

Tony listened to Claire explain that she had an errand, that the gallery door was supposed to be locked, and Jimmy was supposed to have been opening crates in the back. He heard Kate tell a uniformed officer what had happened, but fury enveloped him as he scanned her torn blouse, the tendrils of hair hanging in disarray around her face, the redness and inflammation on the flesh at her wrist.

He wanted to make these moments easier for her and felt a dull, overbearing heaviness weighing him down because he couldn't share more. No man could quite comprehend that degree of physical vulnerability, of humiliation. All he could do was offer the one thing he sensed she lacked at that moment—his strength.

As the officer turned to leave, Claire tightened her grip on Kate's shoulders. "When the police get him, I plan on giving him a piece of my mind."

Kate heard fierce maternal indignation, which frightened her even more. She gripped her mother's arm. "Stay away from him. I'm fine," she added, trying to downplay the incident. She didn't trust Jimmy Foster.

"Claire, listen to her," Tony insisted.

Kate looked at him. Could he read minds? she wondered. She heard a soothing softness in his voice as if he knew how important such calmness was.

Through sheer willpower Kate managed a parting smile for her mother, but throughout the drive to her apartment a knot still constricted her throat, warning her that she was teetering on the brink of tears again. Exhaustion threatened to overcome her, and she had to struggle against the urge to close her eyes and sleep and, most of all, forget.

She entered her apartment with Tony, but still the ringing of the phone rattled her. Kate bolted. The reaction seemed ridiculous, but she couldn't quell her inner unsteadiness. For a long moment she stared at the phone, annoyed by the idea that she was frightened of an inanimate object. Finally she grabbed the receiver. "Hello."

"Guess who?"

She knew she paled. Was any woman ever prepared for that one particular voice from her past? She doubted she would have ever been ready to hear Gary's voice again. But she didn't need this—tonight of all nights.

Tony was beside her in two strides. "Who?" he asked quietly.

Kate slowly wagged her head. "Not Jimmy," she assured him in a low voice.

The male voice purred into her ear through the receiver. "I'm back in town for a few days. I'd like to see you. And your mother," he added, as if such a gracious gesture would clinch her acceptance.

She felt nothing, not even the pain. "I don't see any point in that."

"Ever pragmatic." The voice grew lower, softened, reviving a memory of nighttime and gentle caresses. "I'd find the idea of seeing you again exciting."

She could visualize him slouched in a chair, his lips curving in a cocky grin. Kate wanted to snap at him, but saw Tony studying her closely, searchingly. Could any one day get worse? she wondered. Why didn't she just hang up on him?

"We could meet for old times' sake," Gary went on. "You remember old times, don't you?"

She was his latest whim, she realized. For some selfish, inconceivable reason, he wanted to win back his wife. "What do you want?"

"Isn't that obvious?"

"Not interested," she said, amazed by her quiet tone, considering all she'd endured. With the same quiet calm she set down the receiver, cutting off whatever he was saying. She felt no ache, just relief. He no longer meant anything to her. "A voice from the past." She shrugged and gave Tony her best attempt at a blasé look. "Gary."

He sent her a lopsided smile that looked strained. "The ex-Mr. Wonderful?"

"He never was Mr. Wonderful," she assured him. "Gary said the right words and smiled the perfect, irresistible smiles at the right moments, but he never really cared. He never knew how to care about anyone but himself."

As she scurried into the bedroom to change clothes, Tony felt his token smile give way to a frown. He could see how much she hurt, a deep, penetrating kind of hurt, one that went beyond simply loving and losing.

He wasn't like her ex. She realized that, didn't she? Much as he wanted to believe she did, he knew she still harbored a fair amount of mistrust, yet couldn't think of any way—not one damn way—to convince her that he was different.

As she returned to the room, a carryall bag dangling from her hand, helplessness gnawed at him. He wanted to curse, but didn't. As if magnetized, his eyes cut to the bruise on her wrist. She'd already been through too much today. Uttering a quiet oath, he closed the distance between them, then gently touched the purple stain. "Bad, huh?"

Kate stifled a wince. "It's nothing."

He opened his arms to her. "It's been a hell of a day."

Giving in to her exhaustion, Kate accepted his embrace and pressed herself against him. He was becoming a rock of strength she'd never expected to find, had never thought she would cling to.

With the caution and gentleness of touching something fragile, he framed her face with his hands and kissed her tenderly, as if it were the one gesture he knew she would need most of all. He murmured softly against her cheek. "What can I do to make it a better one?"

She trembled despite her determination to be strong. "Just hold me," she requested. "Just hold me."

Tony smoothed back her hair in a comforting gesture, then drew her close. No more words would help; he guessed that she didn't want sympathy. He knew she wouldn't accept a lot of things from him. But then not all of her bruises were visible ones.

It was after midnight before she fell asleep. Still holding her, Tony lay awake at two in the morning. He slept fitfully and awoke several more times before light crept into the bedroom. Expecting the buzz of the alarm clock, he tensed as the telephone rang.

Kate wiggled, shifting, and murmured groggily. "Do you want me to answer it?"

He shot her a puzzled look.

As she motioned toward the telephone, she teased, "Daydreaming?" Relieved to hear the familiar lightness in her voice, he pressed his lips to her cheek as she cuddled closer. "About you."

"Smooth talker."

Her words cut through him. At that moment he felt like one, a dishonest one, but couldn't bring himself to tell her about yesterday's conversation with his father.

"You could let it ring," Kate urged, pushing her length against him and draping one leg over his.

As she curled toward him, he found his face buried in the sweet-scented mass of her hair and fumbled to dislodge the receiver from its cradle. "Can you do that?" he murmured.

She released a self-deprecating sigh. "Never."

As her lips caressed his ear, he had to make himself remember that the receiver was in his hand.

"Tony?"

He stopped his lazy caress of Kate's hip and concentrated on his father's voice.

"Is your sister there?"

"Pop, what's the matter?"

"I didn't do right by her."

Grimacing, Tony pushed himself up on one elbow, not needing a great deal of explanation to know that Teresa had finally announced her divorce. "She told you?"

"And I lost my temper."

For a moment Tony's mind went blank, then he slowly visualized the scene between father and daughter. "Pop, you didn't blame her?"

"You think I would do that?" his father shouted, audibly irritated. "Never! But I was busy and she was looking for a hug and I kept asking questions. Questions that hurt her." He said something in Italian, a word Tony had learned early in life because he knew he wasn't supposed to. "Did you know he was seeing other women?" his father asked, by now unable to rein in his anger.

Tony straightened his back. "Damn him."

Kate propped her chin on one hand and frowned.

"No," Tony answered, aware by Kate's concerned look that he wasn't cloaking his fury. "I didn't know. She told you that?"

"Yes. She caught him with some woman at a party."

"Is that what caused—?"

"No," his father cut in. "That happened months ago. She stayed with him—stayed because she knew I would be upset if she gave up on the marriage. Tony—Tony, what did I do to her? She was unhappy for too long," he said with a troubled sigh. "She should have left that no-good—"

"Calm down, Pop."

"She should have left him sooner," Luigi went on, with a certainty that Tony knew his father wanted him to convey to Teresa. "I wish I could tell her so, but I called her house. She isn't home."

"Was he?"

"No. The baby-sitter answered my call."

Tony relaxed a little. "Okay. Don't worry about her then."

"How can you tell me not to worry?" his father yelled.

"Because she hasn't gone too far," Tony assured him. "She'd never go too far from Sara. I'll find her."

"Yes, yes," his father said, as if reassuring himself. "And call me?"

"I will."

Kate waited until he set down the receiver. "There's a problem?"

He ran a hand over the knotted muscles at the back of his neck. "My sister." He swung his legs out of bed. "I have to find her."

"She's gone?"

He shrugged as he tugged on his jeans. "I don't know, but I don't think so. I think that she needed some time alone to think. But Pop doesn't know where she is. I have to find her," he repeated, grabbing a shirt. "I have to go, but—" He stopped abruptly, dropping to his knees and hunting under the bed for his sneakers. Straightening, he stared at Kate's still-flushed face. She looked more than inviting. Enticing. Bewitching. She made him want to crawl back into bed and think about nothing but the two of them. "You okay?"

He bent closer and she framed his face with her hands. "I'm okay."

He kissed her lightly. "I'll see you later." He started to turn away, then paused and looked back at her once more. "You'll be here?" Kate nodded.

With her nod, he hurried out the door. Kate scrambled out of bed and watched from a window as he jumped into his truck and pulled away.

Kate felt edgy. She'd seen worry in his eyes and wished she could have offered him the solace he'd given her the night before.

Chapter Eleven

Tony spent the morning and early afternoon calling Teresa's friends and visiting her regular haunts, including an exclusive lingerie shop.

"Yes, Mrs. Harmon was here," the saleswoman told him, "but that was hours ago."

Relieved that his sister was releasing pent-up tension with a shopping spree, he drove back to her house and parked his car. An arm draped over the steering wheel, he waited.

When she finally drove into the driveway late that afternoon, he stalled for another fifteen minutes until the baby-sitter left.

Teresa flung open the door with no pretense of a smile. No tears streamed down her cheeks. Her features pinched, she looked ready for battle. "I thought you were Jon," she said by way of excuse, whirling away and leaving him standing in the doorway.

Tony slammed the door behind him and charged into the room on her heels. "Where have you been? What are you doing? Pop is worrying himself sick about you."

She faced him with a pained look. "I didn't mean to make him worry. I went shopping."

"What the hell, Teresa?"

"Stop yelling," she pleaded. "Why are you here?"

He stepped closer. "I'm worried, too," he admitted.

"Don't be."

He didn't buy her assumed indifference.

"I stopped crying over him months ago." Her shoulders sagged. "But I feel so bad that I let Sara down—and Papa."

She looked frail, even breakable, Tony reflected.

"Papa didn't understand," she said with a shake of her head.

Tony swore softly, using an earthy word that made her swivel back and arch a brow at him. "Ah, Peaches."

"Tony!" she wailed upon hearing the childhood nickname, and despite the tears welling into her eyes, affectionately punched his arm. "You haven't called me that in years."

"Come on, Sis. Jon was a pain in the ass."

Though it seemed like an effort, she smiled. "Then why do I feel like such a failure?"

"You didn't do anything wrong. Pop told me that Jon was running around."

She yanked a tissue from the box on the coffee table, revealing that she wasn't as much in control as she pretended to be. "Tony, you really don't see me too realistically. No marriage ends because of only one person," Teresa said raggedly. "We both made mistakes. Jon just made his first." Clutching the tissue, she plopped onto the sofa. "But I made mistakes, too," she admitted with a weak smile. "I pushed him, Tony. I put too much pressure on our marriage."

He sat down beside her, closing his hand over the baby's rattle that lay nearby. He toyed with it as he reviewed mental images of his sister. She was placid by nature, the only tranquil one in a family of gregarious, sometimes overbearing people. She'd never made waves. She was an anchor, solid and not easily swayed. "I doubt that."

"No, it's true. I never gave us the time we needed. He didn't want a child. I pushed for that, too. I had a baby, hoping it would hold our marriage together. I don't regret having Sara," she assured him quickly with a shake of her head. "She means everything to me. But I broke the trust. I was at fault, too. And I did it because I thought I could make something strong that wasn't." She held the tissue so tightly in her palm that he saw her knuckles grow pale. "You can't force love. It either is or it isn't. And Jon and I never had the strong, trusting kind of love that makes a marriage last forever."

Dodging his stare, she leaned forward to fiddle with the flowers that stood in a short brass container on the coffee table. "I thought a baby might make a difference," she told him, meeting his eyes again.

Tony set down the rattle and slipped a hand over hers. He couldn't understand a man who would reject his own flesh and blood. "He's a fool."

"I've thought of worse names," she said with a strained giggle. "But I learned something. There are no guarantees with marriage. It's commitment of the heart that really counts. Without it there's nothing."

"No, there isn't." As tears brightened her eyes, he draped a protective arm around her narrow shoulders. No, there isn't, he repeated silently. Tony agonized for her and suddenly for himself, as well. The ache intensified. Holding his sister tightly to him, he leaned back against the sofa cushion. He'd been stupid, he realized. Stupid.

His little sister had just taught her big brother a lesson in living. He needed permanency. He wanted marriage and a family again. He'd placed a lot of value on both throughout his life, but without love, marriages fell apart and children were hurt. Only love made a relationship work.

But he'd kept himself from saying too much about love and marriage to Kate, even though he'd felt the need for both. As he stared at Teresa, he watched her battling the failure of a marriage. She'd lost something that she'd hoped for—a dream. It had slipped from her grasp. Well, his own had, too, on that fatal night when Michelle and Joey had died.

Tony had thought he'd come to terms with that loss. Now awareness grew that he never really had. After losing the two people he'd first loved, he'd been afraid to take the final step that would bind him and Kate to each other. It was ironic, he realized, that the chains associated with marriage didn't guarantee anything. Loss was always possible. It was a part of loving someone.

"Tony?"

He focused on his sister again. "Thanks," he said softly.

He saw her brows draw together. "For what?"

"For reminding me that love is a risk worth taking."

The scent of pines and the sight of the amusement park were becoming as familiar as home to Kate.

She turned into the driveway that led to the park and flipped down the car's visor. The sun hung low on the horizon, glinting off one of the rides, so that even with her sunglasses on, the glare was almost unbearable.

Walking from her car to the building Tony called home, she kept her head bent and her eyes on the ground. A key in one hand, Kate juggled a grocery bag as she opened the door. Oddly, it seemed more like home to her now than her own apartment did.

She entered, kicked off her shoes, then strolled toward the kitchen.

Tony stayed with his sister longer than he'd planned. The sun had set by the time he strolled from his car to his home. For the first time in years he felt at peace with himself. And a touch obsessed with the woman whose car was parked nearby.

He opened the door, aching for the sight of Kate. One step in, he caught the scent of food cooking and saw her standing at the stove. "What's this?"

A knife held tightly in her hand, she whipped around. Though she looked calm, he saw her draw a deep breath. "I almost skewered you with a paring knife."

"It smells wonderful in here," he said, pushing away from the doorjamb.

"You aren't the only whiz kid in the kitchen."

As he drew her close, her sweet fragrance overshadowed every other scent. "No." He inhaled deeply. "You smell wonderful."

She seemed complacent, willing to stay nestled against him and let their dinner burn. "Tell me what happened."

"First, what are we eating?"

"Its a surprise."

"Give me a hint."

Kate drew back and peered into his eyes. It was impossible to see them, since he was still wearing mirrored sunglasses, but she noted his frown.

"Are you trying to decide what it's called?" he teased.

Kate wrinkled her nose. "Pork chops. I'm making pork chops."

"Let me shower and then I'll help you."

As he started to draw away, Kate grabbed his hand to stop him. "What about your sister?"

"She's okay." We both are, he thought to himself, appreciating her concern. Before the night was over, he planned to tell her just how much she really meant to him.

In the manner of someone judging a painting, Kate reared back her head and studied him. "What's with the shades then?" She tapped a fingernail at the corner of his glasses.

Using a knuckle, Tony nudged them onto the bridge of his nose. "I'm an international film star incognito."

Kate laughed then. "The paparazzi were too much for you?"

"It had become dull," he said, feigning an arrogant shrug before turning toward the door.

"So you've been looking for excitement of a different kind?" she suggested.

He shot a glance over his shoulder and winked. "And found it."

"Silly man," she muttered to herself, and was still smiling when the telephone rang minutes later.

"Is this Kate?" a man asked in response to her greeting.

She tried to place the voice. "Yes."

"Kate, this is Tony's papa. Is he there?"

"Yes, he just came home."

He sighed worriedly. "Did he find her? He must have," he said, as if reassuring himself. "Maybe I should call her."

"Don't you want to talk to him first?"

"Yes, yes," he said, seeming too preoccupied to think clearly. "Where could she have gone all day?"

"I'm sure that she just went out for a while. I always go shopping for shoes when I'm—I'm uneasy," Kate said, careful not to upset him more than he obviously was.

"Yes, yes. She must have done that. I thank the good Lord that Tony didn't leave for California yet."

"California?" As Kate repeated the word, she fought the knot in her throat. Tightening her fingers on the receiver, she felt her heart hammering a hard, painful beat.

"If he had been gone already, I don't know what I would have done. If Teresa is upset, she always wants to talk to him. She always talked to him when something bothered her. She always was close to him. She..." He stopped, as if not knowing what else to say. "Forgive me for bothering you, Kate. Just an old man rambling," he said, clearly forcing a lighter note.

Her throat dry, she tried to swallow the lump lodged there. "That's all right," she assured him, her eyes straying to Tony standing in the bedroom doorway in a bathrobe. "Your father," she said simply before she said goodbye to Luigi.

Smiling, he reached for the telephone receiver and made a grab for her. Kate dodged him and brushed off his arm. She wanted to get away, wanted time, needed distance to think clearly. Her back to him, she caught fragments of what he was saying to his father, but his words were muffled.

She'd done it again, she thought agonizingly. She'd given her heart away. When would she learn? She squeezed her eyes shut, trying to fight the ache he'd awakened. She hated surprises. She truly had never liked them.

Tony stared at the straightness of her slender back while he answered his father's questions. With the same sense of pending doom that made a person watch a dark sky for a tornado, he felt anxiety rippling through him. Then she turned her head to face him and he saw how pale she'd grown. He saw that her banker's mask was back in place, her eyes a cool gray like a foreboding winter sky. And he saw the doubts in them.

He managed a quick goodbye to his father and crossed to her. He wasn't a man to dodge a confrontation. He reached out to caress her hair, wanting to reassure himself that he was misreading the emotion in her eyes. When she jerked away, he knew he wasn't. "What is this?"

Kate inched back a few steps, using the coffee table as a protective barrier. She wanted to scream as her mind raced with unreasonable anger, as it warned her of the loneliness she would feel without him.

"What did I miss?" Tony racked his brain to guess what his father might have innocently said to her to set her off. He held his arms out, palms up in a gesture of appeal. "I had a warm, smiling woman minutes ago. What did Pop say to you?"

He saw her stiffen. "He told me that you're going to California."

He reared back as if she'd hit him. God, he could lose her, he realized in that instant.

"When were you planning to announce it? Were you just going to desert your plans for the amusement park? Were you going to say, 'Look, Kate, it's been nice, but I'm leaving for a while'?" Kate felt no confidence, no certainty that she wasn't making a mistake. She only knew that she'd heard those words before and had vowed never to hear them again.

"Kate..."

"You don't have to make excuses." Her voice remained calm, but was hot with accusation.

"Because you don't care?"

"That's not what counts anymore."

"What does?"

"I don't want another fair-weather relationship."

"Fair—?" Tony almost laughed. "What the hell are you talking about?" Circling the coffee table, he closed the distance between them.

"What does it sound like?"

"It sounds like you won't give us a chance, will you? Did you ever plan to?" he demanded, battling his own temper.

"Neither of us expected more," she retorted, aware that she lied.

"I did," he said simply.

"Until you left?" she demanded almost defiantly.

Tony retaliated like a blind man, jabbing at anything to defend himself. "Dammit, not every man is your ex."

"He's in the past," she claimed.

He heard the fury in her tone, the kind that spoke of bitter hurt, and knew he'd hit the target. "Only dead ghosts stay buried, Kate. Your ex-husband isn't."

She spun away, shaking her head.

"Don't," he said softly, trying his utmost not to yell. "He stands between us, haunting our relationship. But I'm not him." Suddenly he felt awkward, unsure of what he was really up against, wishing he knew what the right words were for this moment. "I won't—"

She raised her hands to ward off any speeches. "Don't make promises. I know about promises. When I needed the man who'd promised love, I was alone." To her own amazement, her voice sounded steady. "I believe in actions, not words. Gary's promises meant nothing."

Tony braced himself. He could still make everything work for them, but he had to stay calm. Most of all he needed to know what he was fighting. "Why didn't they?"

As he moved closer, Kate withdrew. Her throat felt raw with suppressed tears, but she couldn't give in, couldn't stand more broken promises.

"Why?" he demanded again, angry and frustrated.

"He couldn't handle life's darker side." She heard her voice crack and fought the weakness rushing at her. He was forcing her to recall a time in her life when the days had been filled with anger, disappointment and dread. "He couldn't even come to the hospital."

He drew a quiet breath with difficulty as uncertainty floated over him. "Hospital?"

Kate swallowed hard and spun around. "Hospitals bothered him. Everything bothered him," she said with a trace of the anguish she'd once felt. She'd given someone her heart and he'd offered nothing in return. "Within days after my initial visit to the doctor, he came home and told me that he'd been hired to work with this crew. It meant going to Le Mans. He wasn't seeking adventure. He scurried away...." She knew she was close to falling apart and placed a palm upon her chest. "Ran. He ran." She struggled to keep her voice calm. "He ran from a lump on the breast." Something ripped the words from her. "Small and benign. But he ran. He imagined horrors that I hadn't allowed myself to consider. He saw the big C." She raised her voice. "He saw chemotherapy. He saw his wife retching over a toilet bowl, losing her hair, turning into a skeleton of her former self.''

Tony released a ragged breath. "That son of a bitch. He told you that?" he asked, so quickly that the words seemed to hang in the air like a whisper.

"In so many words." Tears stung her eyes. All the old wrath and resentment of those days absorbed her again. "He was sorry that he wouldn't be here for me. But when he came back, I'd be through with all of that *stuff*. We could go on as before. He failed the great big test, the one where the person doesn't just say love," she said harshly, her throat threatening to close. "It's the one where a person shows love by sticking around and being near for the other person when he's needed."

"And you think I won't do that?" he challenged.

"When I needed him, he wasn't there."

Tony took a chance and stepped closer. As she drew back, he stopped in midstride. "I'll be there," he promised, holding out his arms to her.

She wanted to cling to his words, to believe everything he was saying. But she knew better, didn't she? "Gary made promises, too. People make promises, then they walk away from them!" she yelled, sweeping up her purse.

As she raced to the door, Tony ran after her. He'd found the woman he needed, the woman who'd become his life. "Kate, wait," he appealed.

His words seemed to have fallen on deaf ears. Hurrying, she rushed out without giving him even one last look.

Tony was at a loss. What the hell could he do now? Clenching a fist, he wanted to punch something. He'd let her go without finishing the fight, but her rejection had stunned him. He wondered how he could reason with her when he could barely keep a grasp upon sanity himself. Weariness engulfed him. His fault. This was his fault. Silently he swore at himself, wondering how he could have been so stupid. He knew her uncertainties, her suspicions.

They'd gone so far, but not nearly far enough, he reasoned. There were no words to obliterate her doubts about him. She would believe the worse of him at the slightest provocation. Trust. They were talking about trust, the unspoken kind that mingled with love, that made a person know the other one would be there for them.

He didn't know how to convince her, he realized as he slid into his car. He'd lost contact during those few moments when he'd stared into eyes too cool, listened to a voice too emotionless to belong to the woman he cared about.

Love was never easy, he reminded himself. Never.

He swore softly, hating the man from her past who had treated her gentle heart so carelessly.

* * *

Kate fought the sting of tears behind her eyes, trying to persuade herself that she'd handled plenty of disappointments before. But even hours of driving didn't put distance between her and her feelings for Tony.

By the time she slipped her key into the lock of her apartment door, she felt so drained that she was surprised she even noticed that the lock didn't click.

Panic seized her, then abated. She stepped into the living room—and saw her mother poised on the edge of a sofa cushion.

Claire gave Kate only enough time to slip off her shoes and plug in the coffee brewer. "What happened, Katie?"

Kate didn't want to know the name of her mother's spy.

The silk fabric of her mother's dress rustled as she crossed her legs. "Explain to me why this happened," she said in a tolerant tone that reminded Kate of her youth.

Kate shook her head and strolled back to the kitchen. Her chest ached as if something heavy were resting on it. She stalled for time, pouring herself a cup of coffee.

She closed her eyes, wanting to sag onto a chair and rest her head on the table. She was tired, yet knew she wouldn't sleep.

At the burning sensation of tears, she blinked hard. She'd get her life back to normal. She'd forget him.

Her heart thudded painfully as she faced the hard fact that she would never forget him. He'd made her dream again. He'd made her open her heart and love again. She swallowed a tightness in her throat.

Trudging back into the living room, she found her mother still perched on the sofa. In her usual prodding manner, Claire insisted, "You broke it off, didn't you?"

Kate decided on a direct approach. "Yes, I did. I should have sooner, but I was foolish." Restless, she crossed the room and straightened some magazines on a table.

"Katie, you weren't foolish."

"Mother, he's going to California, so don't try to defend him." She shook her head to banish the faint inkling of doubt about her own decision. "I can't depend on him. He's no different than—"

"Than Gary?" Sighing in exasperation, Claire dropped her purse onto the sofa cushion. "Katie, you're grasping at straws! You're not giving him a chance."

At the sadness clouding her mother's eyes, Kate looked away and stared out the window. She heard the chime of the doorbell, the rustle of silk as her mother moved from the sofa to answer it.

"That's Larry," her mother murmured, standing near. "I hope you don't mind, but I asked him to pick me up here."

Kate drew a calming breath and forced herself to focus on her mother.

"I'm driving him to the airport," she offered as an explanation. "Someone in Texas is interested in his wood carvings."

Kate smiled ruefully. So she'd been wrong about the Bola tie man.

"If you need me, I'll be at Louisa's later." Clutching her purse, her mother paused in passing. "Everyone deserves another chance. Don't you, too?" she whispered.

Feeling numb, Kate sat still and quiet in a room darkening with nightfall. None of the questions she asked herself were gentle or kind.

Suddenly she raced into the bathroom. Her hand on the aspirin bottle, she heard the phone ringing. She didn't bother to run for it and heard her message ramble out of the answering machine. Facing the bathroom mirror for what seemed like minutes, she finally tossed two aspirins into her mouth and scooped water into her palm to wash them down.

The headache throbbed. It wasn't unbearable, just an annoying, dull ache that wouldn't ease up. Splashing water onto her face, she welcomed its cool relief and waited, letting the moisture drip over her jaw before she patted her face dry.

Sighing, she flicked off the light and reentered the living room to switch on the answering machine. She sank onto a cushion, praying she wouldn't hear Tony's voice, but her mother's feminine one greeted her instead.

"Someone broke into the gallery, Kate. Security called me. I'm going there to check on it."

Kate frowned, wishing her mother would show more caution. Wishing she had demonstrated some herself.

Time seemed to stand still. Somehow she would put her life back together. She would reach a time when her heart didn't ache. But that time wasn't now.

Tony had been pacing the office of his father's restaurant for the past hour and a half, waiting for Claire's call. After Kate had left him, he'd driven to her apartment and had nearly gone crazy when he hadn't seen her car in the parking lot. At a loss, he'd driven to the restaurant and called Claire. When Claire had finally called from the airport five minutes ago, sounding rushed, she'd rattled out something about her gallery, then told him that Kate was home. Tony had heard a sadness in her voice that offered no encouragement.

As he slid back into his car now and flicked on the ignition, he was angry. Angry and frustrated. He sensed what Claire hadn't said. Kate hadn't listened to her.

He fought his darkening mood. He couldn't let macho anger grab ahold. He couldn't let taut nerves snap. But he couldn't dodge an almost self-defensive urge to say, "To hell with it! To hell with all of this!" She should have been at his house, should have been in his arms right now.

Minutes later he jabbed at the doorbell as if it were the enemy. Logic no longer controlled him. It didn't go hand in hand with love.

As she opened the door, back rigid, chin raised, even her stance irritated him until he saw the tears brightening her eyes. Anger he could have battled, but the hurt unnerved him. "We need to talk," he insisted calmly, but his voice sounded harder than he'd intended.

Hesitant, she drew back, stopped, released her grip on the doorknob, then stepped away to move to the middle of her living room. But the door remained open. He stared at her slender back and gauged what to do next. He'd grown familiar with her stubbornness.

"There's nothing to say."

"Yes, there is." His words came out clipped as he fought tenderness and the urge to crawl to her. "I am going to California, but only for a few days."

Kate stood perfectly still, unsure what he was trying to promise her.

"This isn't the way that I planned to say it." Tony sighed heavily. "I told Pop that I wouldn't manage the opening of the restaurant in California for him. I should have told you," he admitted. "But I've been holding back. Holding back from telling you what I really feel. Holding back from telling you that you're everything to me." He stepped forward, hands outstretched in an appeal for understanding. "I love you, Kate."

Because he'd never said those words before, she wasn't prepared for them. Why now? Her heart twisting, she breathed hard and felt close to tears. Oh, God, how she wanted to believe in him! She truly loved him and was shocked at the realization; she'd never planned to give so much of herself again.

"Did you hear me?" At her silence, he felt panic instead of annoyance. "Say something." Tony fought his own frustration. "Kate." Calmly, steadily, he offered her a hand.

"Oh, God, don't," she pleaded softly, jerking away before he could touch her. She still stood straight, her back stiff. "I don't know." The words came out with a ragged sob as she fought the knot in her throat.

They stood facing each other for a long moment, the silence lingering, clinging to the air.

At the sharp trill of the telephone, Kate jumped; the ringing filled the room with a sound more startling than an explosion. On a harsh breath, she whirled around and snatched up the receiver to stop the noise.

"Oh, my God!" Nothing in life prepared a person for the inconceivable, she thought, for the moments that passed swiftly and lingered for ever. Nothing prepared a person for pain, either. She listened to the male voice at the other end and almost collapsed.

Chapter Twelve

Tony rushed forward as she reached for something to steady herself.

Kate dodged the dizziness closing in on her. The caller's message was short. One sentence. She listened to the dial tone and knew she was holding a dead receiver, but couldn't make her body respond to her mind's command to move.

Tony crossed the room in two strides. He started to reach for her, then stopped himself, halted by the glazed, haunted look in her eyes. "What's the matter?"

Kate suppressed hysteria, clutching the receiver so tightly in her hand that when he leaned over and lifted it from her fingers, her hand remained cramped in a clawlike curve. Paralyzed by fear, she didn't know what to do. "Mother..."

He hesitated again before touching her hand. It felt cold, lifeless. "What?" he demanded.

"He has..."

At the sound of desperation he could hear in her voice, he grabbed her upper arms. "Talk, dammit!" he snapped, shaking her.

"At the gallery. Jimmy has my mother." Kate trembled and swayed toward him. Breathless, motionless, she stifled a whimper. "He has my mother, Tony," she said, feeling panic rising within her. "He's threatened to kill her if..." She swallowed. "Tony, he wants money, or..."

He tightened his grip to keep her from rushing away. "All right, all right. Calm down," he said sharply. None too gently, he pushed her onto the cushion of a chair. "How much money?"

Kate struggled with the answer. She whispered a figure that seemed astronomical, darting her eyes to the clock. It was nine-thirty at night. She couldn't get a dime more than she had in the apartment. How much was that? She labored frantically to remember how much cash she had in her purse. Forty-three dollars. She had some hidden, too, she remembered. Emergency money. Another hundred. But...

She felt bile rush into her throat and swallowed. "What are you doing?"

Head bent, he jabbed a finger at the numbers on the telephone. "Calling the police."

She bolted from the cushion. "He said no police. He said—"

As she wrestled with him for the receiver, he blocked her with one shoulder and rattled off information.

Adrenaline pumping through her, she gasped for breath, her lungs heaving. She had to think consciously about the act of breathing, certain if she didn't that she would allow herself another moment of panic and forget to breathe altogether.

"Come on."

He grabbed her arm and felt Kate balk.

"Move, Kate," he said fiercely, then as if she were a small child who was slow to understand, he spoke in a measured manner. "Be logical. We have to stall him."

"We can't pay him—we have to pay him," she said, contradicting herself.

She charged with him out of the building and toward his car. Hysteria threatened to engulf her. She battled it. She had to think clearly, to stay calm.

She said nothing when he stopped, dashed into his father's restaurant and then rushed out, a cloth money bag dangling from his hands. Imagined terrors flashed in Kate's mind. "What will I do if I lose her?"

"You won't," he answered, flicking on the ignition. Tires squealed as the car shot out of the parking lot and onto the street. She clung to the bag, twisting the fabric between her hands. Nothing had ever prepared her for this hellish kind of nightmare. The safe, comfortable life she'd established during the past three years was slipping away without warning.

As Tony braked the car, a sick sense of dread consumed her. She scrambled for control, hit the door, and bolted. Rain pelted onto her head and her arms, but she ignored the downpour. Its cool caress offered welcome relief from the perspiration drenching her.

Feet from the gallery door, she was jarred to a standstill and pushed aside by the hard jolt of Tony's hip. Though he shouted something, his voice drifted to her as if she were standing at the opposite end of a long tunnel. Frantic, she shoved at his chest. "Let me go!"

"Don't be a damn fool! You can't just rush in there."

"He has my mother. I have to go in there. I can't lose her. You don't understand. I can't..." Words failed her as his eyes met hers. Kate saw in his gaze what she'd ignored for too long. He understood. No one could suffer through his nightmare of sorrow and not understand desperation and helplessness. "Tony, I have to help her," she pleaded. "I have—"

"We'll get her out," he said firmly. "He wants this," he reminded her, yanking the money bag from her fingers.

Shifting his body, his shoulder brushing hers, he gave her no chance to challenge him. He stepped ahead, blocking her path. Kate heard the soft wail of a siren in the distance and prayed the police would hurry. As Tony pushed open the door, the buzzer droned, seeming to echo off the walls and mingle with the roar filling her ears.

A hand on his back, she felt his muscles tense. She stood motionless, too, sucking in a breath as she saw her mother. An unbearable weight suddenly burdened her. She swayed, her knees weakening. She'd never fainted in her life. But then, she'd never seen such terror on her mother's face before.

Always so meticulous, her mother looked unkempt, her hair tangled, her wide, expressive eyes glazed with fear. As Jimmy bent her arm up behind her and yanked her toward him, she winced. At her halfhearted struggle he spewed out a harsh, vile curse and snaked an arm across her throat.

Kate froze and swallowed fear so real that she could taste its acrid flavor.

The knife blade angled beneath her mother's jaw glinted in the overhead lights. The steel looked abrasive and foreign in the room filled with her mother's photographs and peaceful pastel paintings.

A hand to her mouth, Kate muffled her gasp. Fury urged her to lunge at him, but Tony blocked her and inched a step closer.

"We brought the money. Let her go."

Sweat dotted Jimmy's face. "If you move, I cut her," he promised.

Kate smothered hysteria at the sight of the knife's sharp edge against her mother's flesh. She couldn't imagine a more horrible sight.

Brave men are sometimes cowards, Tony thought. He would feel the blood of a gentle woman staining his hands if he made a mistake. And it seemed so easy to make one. Don't think. Don't think about too much, he told himself. "Here's the money. Now let her go."

At the shrill of sirens, his hand trembling, Jimmy shot a quick, excited glance toward the door behind them.

Tony forced the final moment. "You haven't got much time. I'll give you the bag after you let her go." His voice remained low, emotionless, and brooked no other option.

With a panicky look toward the door, Jimmy loosened his punishing grip and moved the hand that held the knife to Claire's shoulder.

It was the move Tony had hoped for. He tossed the bag out of Jimmy's reach. As he lunged for it, Tony jumped forward. Striking like a cornered cat, Jimmy lashed out with the knife. On a harsh breath, Tony ducked the blade. Crouched, he wasted no time and dived at Jimmy's stomach, doubling him over.

As he stumbled back, Tony tumbled with him. They bumped into a counter, their arms sliding across its top and sweeping off a framed photograph. Glass shattered and fell to the floor, crunching beneath them.

Kate leaped toward her mother. As if magnetized, they came together hard, her mother sagging against her. In terror, they watched as Tony's arm rose as one with Jimmy's in a struggle for the knife.

Muttered curses, the sound of their harsh breathing, the shuffling of their feet filled the room.

An eternity seemed to pass before the door flew open. A scream for help lodged in Kate's throat as she fixed her eyes on the rush of men in blue uniforms.

They closed in, blocking Kate's view. Sounds merged—the clatter of the knife, the snap of handcuffs, the authoritative tone of a policeman. Finally she saw Tony rolling away.

Safe. He was safe. It was her only thought as she watched an officer pull him to his feet. Kate reassured herself that he hadn't been hurt. As he staggered back, his face bathed in sweat, she took a step, her hand out to reach for him, to touch him. But he turned his back, and the real weight of her own foolishness bore down upon her.

He nodded in response to a policeman's question and moved in unison with him toward the door. Another officer stood near her mother. He said something, words that Kate couldn't comprehend. Her mind heard only one word. Fool. She was a fool.

"Where's Tony?"

Kate met her mother's eyes. Wide with alarm, they pinned Kate. "He wasn't hurt, was he?"

"No, he wasn't hurt." Kate spoke in an agonized whisper. "He's gone."

"Gone?"

Kate struggled not to cry. "Mother, it's over."

* * *

At Kate's insistence, her mother agreed to stay for the night. It was a restless one while Kate struggled to pull herself together, searching for logic.

Exhausted, she dragged herself from bed the next morning. She considered burying her head beneath the pillow until the ache inside her subsided, but such behavior would be childish and futile. Feeling as if she were in limbo, paralyzed by some invisible force, she moved on legs that felt like lead as she showered and dressed for work.

Ambling into the kitchen, Kate heard the morning-radio newscaster rattling off brief details about the incident at the gallery. While he spoke matter-of-factly, Kate doubted that she'd ever forget the ordeal.

"My, they do make it sound traumatic, don't they?" her mother said from her position at the kitchen table.

Kate managed a thin smile. "It was," she reminded her, and flicked the dial to Off.

Claire peered at her over the rim of her coffee cup. "Other things are far more devastating." She reached across the table and clasped Kate's hand. "What does he have to do to prove himself to you, Katie?"

The buzzer sounded, and Kate shot a look toward the door. "Mother, don't," she begged as she felt her throat constrict.

"Oh, Katie." Claire slowly shook her head in a mixture of exasperation and resignation.

Rushing to the door, Kate couldn't deny that she prayed it would be Tony. Instead, she opened the door to a garden assortment of flowers. The man behind the bouquet peeked around the colorful blossoms and grinned at her. It was the Bola tie man. Larry Wilkins gave her his big Texan smile. "Howdy," he said.

Disappointment was like a constricting band across her chest as she opened the door wider to him and murmured a hello in return.

"Larry." Her mother breezed forward with a bright greeting.

He seemed drawn to her. "I heard what happened and flew back," he said in his blustery voice.

Clinging to her pride, Kate hurried to the bedroom, unexpected tears stinging her eyes. She heard a hint of excitement in her mother's voice as she related those heart-stopping moments for Larry. A security guard hadn't called her, she explained. Jimmy had enticed her to the gallery with a lie about a break-in. Kate shook her head in amazement. How did her mother always find the will to turn something so ghastly into an adventure?

Taking a long breath, Kate faced the woman in the mirror honestly. She didn't have much courage. She was afraid. From the beginning she'd been afraid that like her father, like Gary, Tony was the kind of man who ran from reality. She'd been irrational and unreasonable.

The lighthearted man with the dazzling smile who had woven an illusion of moonlight and myth understood that life presented everyone with a fair share of sorrow. Tony wouldn't run when reality snatched away their happily-ever-after ending. He would stand firm beside her to weather the stormy days.

Her mother was right. How many times did she need to see how dependable he was to admit that? He'd revealed an ability to stick by commitments to family and friends over and over again. He'd shown that he was more than a man with a charming smile. When she'd needed him most last night, he'd been beside her all the way.

But she'd looked for a quick exit, a way to leave him first and save herself from heartache.

As if she had no will to stop herself, she moved to the music box he'd given her. Her hand trembled when she reached out to touch it, and she ached at her own stupidity.

She couldn't go on and not do anything. She'd made the biggest mistake of her life and had to correct it.

For the first time in years she reacted on impulse, whirling away from the mirror and toward the telephone. Minutes later she'd finished her call to the bank and had successfully gotten a last-minute vacation day.

"Kate?"

Hearing the voice behind her, Kate said a quick goodbye, set down the receiver and faced her mother.

"He loves you, Katie. Any fool can see that."

"I hear you," she said quietly.

Claire released a soft sigh. "Finally."

Early-morning sunlight glared off the chrome of the Ferris wheel. Tony braced his legs against one of its steel bars while he tightened several bolts, then checked four more. Yanking a rag from his back pocket, he wiped sweat from his face, then dried his hands before beginning the climb down.

How long could he wait to see her again before he went crazy? he wondered. He needed to touch her, but wasn't sure he could set pride aside again. If she didn't love him enough, what was the point?

At the sound of gravel crunching beneath tires, he clutched at the rails around him to steady himself and peered down. His first thought was that his mind was playing tricks on him, and it wasn't Kate's car, that he wasn't watching her. Slowly he began his descent. Only when his feet hit the ground did he weigh the possibilities of why she'd come to see him.

Though all he could remember were the empty hours without her, pride still kept him from moving too close. She'd rejected him. Hell, more than once he'd reached out, only to find himself facing a blank wall.

As he stared at her now, he didn't want to feel that again. But he still ached for her. He couldn't dodge his feelings. He longed to have her in his arms, yet felt as if he were clinging by his fingertips. If they slipped, he would tumble into an abyss that he would never get out of, but he couldn't accept mere moments from her any longer. Always. He needed always. No doubts. No hesitation. He needed her to want him just as steadfastly as he needed her. She had to want him with a certainty that would never allow changing winds to pull them apart.

Kate tried to measure his mood as he strolled slowly toward her. She knew that she had to make the first move. His pride would insist upon it; her love for him demanded it.

Stopping near the merry-go-round, she fought a craving to run to him.

"Is Claire all right?" he asked softly, halting in his turn, his eyes dark and unusually guarded.

She labored for a breath, then answered, "Yes."

"Is there a snag about the loan?"

"No," she whispered. Sunlight beat upon her back. The fragrance of pine drifted over her, yet her world closed in to the space separating them. "Heroes don't get rejected."

He gave a quick, hard, mirthless laugh.

"I've always had a thing for them."

"Do you?"

Kate fought the urge to run and steadied herself with a long breath, shifting her stance and nervously twisting the strap of her purse. "I miss you. I want..." She almost choked on the words, not because she didn't want to say them, but because her life with him hinged on them. "I need you. I need you because I love you."

Slowly his lips curved upward. It was all the encouragement she needed. She moved quickly into the arms that were suddenly open and waiting for her. "I'm so sorry." Sliding her arms around his waist, she flattened herself against him, aching for the closeness.

"I'm sorry, too." He buried his face in her hair. "I honestly didn't realize that marriage suddenly frightened me. It's a hell of a confession, one that I'm not thrilled about having to make. But I didn't want to go through that heartache of loving and losing again any more than you did. Maybe if I'd told you sooner that I love you, none of this would have happened."

She leaned back against the arm tight at her waist and rested a hand upon his shoulder. "I'm not sure if it would have helped," she said, breathing roughly. "I've been running. I always expected you to do that when something unpleasant happened. I wouldn't allow myself to really accept what I felt for you," she said softly.

"But not anymore?"

She shook her head and raised moist eyes to him. "Oh, no. Not anymore. I want to share everything with you." She rushed her words, fearful that if she didn't, she wouldn't say everything she needed to tell him. "I've been afraid, Tony. Afraid that you weren't for real."

"Flesh and blood, Kate." He smiled in a wry, familiar way that tugged at her heart. "Plenty of good and bad traits."

All the feelings bottled within her threatened to burst loose. "More good than bad," she said, fighting tears.

"You don't have to be afraid anymore," he murmured against her cheek. "From now on it's not just you or just me. From now on we face whatever comes our way—good or bad. We do it together."

She closed her eyes and let the softness of his voice float over her. All her life she'd searched for someone like him. And because of her foolishness she'd been afraid to make a commitment, a real one. "Oh, Tony, I can't believe that I nearly lost you," she said raggedly.

He drew her closer. "No, I'd never have let you go. Patellis don't quit without a fight. Some more of Luigi Patelli's wise advice," he said, giving her the smile that she longed to see forever.

Kate touched his cheek and laughed. "I love the way that man thinks."

"What else?"

"I love his son," she said with a smile.

He caught a tear on her cheek with one thumb. "We're halfway home."

Kate frowned. "Only halfway?"

"One more question."

Her heart kicked at the idea that there might be one more thing to keep them apart, then she saw the sparkle of mild amusement in his eyes. "What is it?"

"Will you marry me?"

She wanted to strangle him. Love him. Laughing, she coiled an arm around his neck and nipped at his chin. "I'm not letting you get away."

"No more doubts?" As she shook her head and tightened her arms around him, he grinned broadly. "I'm here for keeps," he whispered against her mouth.

Kate clung to him as if to assure herself she wasn't caught up in a dream, but the mouth on hers was a familiar warm one that was filled with promises of forever.

"Come on," he urged, drawing back to look at her.

Kate pivoted with him toward the trailer, happiness humming within her. "Where are we going?"

"To seal the deal."

Laughing again, her hip tightly pressed to his, she ambled along with him. As she looked up at him, her eyes strayed again to the Ferris wheel. She was down-to-earth. He'd always be up there, reaching for the clouds. But they'd found a place somewhere in between to meet, a place with love, where reality and fantasy mingled.

Her mother had been right all along, she thought, smiling. He was a real charmer, not because he was fun or made her laugh or believe in dreams again. His real charm had come through during all the moments when she'd been able to depend upon him, all the times he'd guessed her fear and still hadn't given up, all those moments when he'd offered her strength or consoling words, and all the times when he'd proved she hadn't been alone to face any real problem that life tossed her way.

When they reached the bottom of the trailer steps, she stopped and scanned the amusement park. "The park looks wonderful," she assured him.

"Not yet." His fingers tightened at the curve of her waist. "But in time."

He'd given her so much. Her heart full of love, she knew of only one gift she could give him in return. "I know what's missing."

Tony looked down at her. Now that he had her close and smiling at him, his world already seemed complete. "What is?"

"A child. Children," she said, taking his face into her hands. "Amusement parks need children."

His eyes grew darker, searching.

Kate leaned toward him. "Our own will love it," she said, then muffled his soft, pleased laugh with a kiss.

*   *   *   *   *

Silhouette Special Edition

COMING NEXT MONTH

#697 NAVY BABY—Debbie Macomber
Hard-living sailor Riley never thought he'd settle down with a preacher's daughter. But he couldn't steer clear of Hannah and their navy baby, though it meant riding out the storm of his life.

#698 SLOW LARKIN'S REVENGE—Christine Rimmer
Local bad boy Winslow Larkin, was back in town . . . and out to seduce the one woman who'd almost tamed his heart years ago. But loving Violet Windemere proved much sweeter than revenge!

#699 TOP OF THE MOUNTAIN—Mary Curtis
The memory of Lili Jamison's high school passion lived on in her love child. Reuniting with Brad Hollingsworth rekindled the actual fire . . . and the guilt of her eleven-year-old secret.

#700 ROMANCING RACHEL—Natalie Bishop
Rachel Stone had her hands full raising her stepson on her own. When strong, stern Tyrrell Rafferty III entered the picture, he completed the family portrait . . . better than she knew!

#701 THE MAN SHE MARRIED—Tracy Sinclair
Teenager Dorian Merrill had fled her hometown and broken marriage to find her fortune. Now the *woman* was back, a penthouse success— but lured to the other side of town by the man she married.

#702 CHILD OF THE STORM—Diana Whitney
When Megan O'Connor lost her beloved sister, she vowed not to lose her seven-year-old nephew. Not even to his father, who resurfaced to claim him . . . and Megan's heart.

AVAILABLE THIS MONTH:

#691 OBSESSION
Lisa Jackson

#692 FAMILY FRIENDLY
Jo Ann Algermissen

#693 THE HEALING TOUCH
Christine Flynn

#694 A REAL CHARMER
Jennifer Mikels

#695 ANNIE IN THE MORNING
Curtiss Ann Matlock

#696 LONGER THAN . . .
Erica Spindler

Silhouette Special Edition

presents

SONNY'S GIRLS

by Emilie Richards, Celeste Hamilton
and Erica Spindler

They had been Sonny's girls, irresistibly drawn to the
charismatic high school football hero. Ten years later, none
could forget the night that changed their lives forever.

In July—
ALL THOSE YEARS AGO by Emilie Richards (SSE #684)
Meredith Robbins had left town in shame. Could she ever banish
the past and reach for love again?

In August—
DON'T LOOK BACK by Celeste Hamilton (SSE #690)
Cyndi Saint was Sonny's steady. Ten years later, she
remembered only his hurtful parting words....

In September—
LONGER THAN... by Erica Spindler (SSE #696)
Bubbly Jennifer Joyce was everybody's friend. But nobody knew
the secret longings she felt for bad boy Ryder Hayes....

"INDULGE A LITTLE" SWEEPSTAKES

HERE'S HOW THE SWEEPSTAKES WORKS

NO PURCHASE NECESSARY

To enter each drawing, complete the appropriate Official Entry Form or a 3" by 5" index card by hand-printing your name, address and phone number and the trip destination that the entry is being submitted for (i.e., Walt Disney World Vacation Drawing, etc.) and mailing it to: Indulge '91 Subscribers-Only Sweepstakes, P.O. Box 1397, Buffalo, New York 14269-1397.

No responsibility is assumed for lost, late or misdirected mail. Entries must be sent separately with first class postage affixed, and be received by: 9/30/91 for the Walt Disney World Vacation Drawing, 10/31/91 for the Alaskan Cruise Drawing and 11/30/91 for the Hawaiian Vacation Drawing. Sweepstakes is open to residents of the U.S. and Canada, 21 years of age or older as of 11/7/91.

For complete rules, send a self-addressed, stamped (WA residents need not affix return postage) envelope to: Indulge '91 Subscribers-Only Sweepstakes Rules, P.O. Box 4005, Blair, NE 68009.

© 1991 HARLEQUIN ENTERPRISES LTD.

DIR-RL

"INDULGE A LITTLE" SWEEPSTAKES

HERE'S HOW THE SWEEPSTAKES WORKS

NO PURCHASE NECESSARY

To enter each drawing, complete the appropriate Official Entry Form or a 3" by 5" index card by hand-printing your name, address and phone number and the trip destination that the entry is being submitted for (i.e., Walt Disney World Vacation Drawing, etc.) and mailing it to: Indulge '91 Subscribers-Only Sweepstakes, P.O. Box 1397, Buffalo, New York 14269-1397.

No responsibility is assumed for lost, late or misdirected mail. Entries must be sent separately with first class postage affixed, and be received by: 9/30/91 for the Walt Disney World Vacation Drawing, 10/31/91 for the Alaskan Cruise Drawing and 11/30/91 for the Hawaiian Vacation Drawing. Sweepstakes is open to residents of the U.S. and Canada, 21 years of age or older as of 11/7/91.

For complete rules, send a self-addressed, stamped (WA residents need not affix return postage) envelope to: Indulge '91 Subscribers-Only Sweepstakes Rules, P.O. Box 4005, Blair, NE 68009.

© 1991 HARLEQUIN ENTERPRISES LTD.

DIR-RL

INDULGE A LITTLE—WIN A LOT!

Summer of '91 Subscribers-Only Sweepstakes

OFFICIAL ENTRY FORM

This entry must be received by: Sept. 30, 1991
This month's winner will be notified by: Oct. 7, 1991
Trip must be taken between: Nov. 7, 1991—Nov. 7, 1992

YES, I want to win the Walt Disney World® vacation for two. I understand the prize includes round-trip airfare, first-class hotel and pocket money as revealed on the "wallet" scratch-off card.

Name _____

Address_____ Apt. _____

City _____

State/Prov. _____ Zip/Postal Code _____

Daytime phone number _____
(Area Code)

Return entries with invoice in envelope provided. Each book in this shipment has two entry coupons—and the more coupons you enter, the better your chances of winning!

© 1991 HARLEQUIN ENTERPRISES LTD.   CPS-M1

INDULGE A LITTLE—WIN A LOT!

Summer of '91 Subscribers-Only Sweepstakes

OFFICIAL ENTRY FORM

This entry must be received by: Sept. 30, 1991
This month's winner will be notified by: Oct. 7, 1991
Trip must be taken between: Nov. 7, 1991—Nov. 7, 1992

YES, I want to win the Walt Disney World® vacation for two. I understand the prize includes round-trip airfare, first-class hotel and pocket money as revealed on the "wallet" scratch-off card.

Name _____

Address_____ Apt. _____

City _____

State/Prov. _____ Zip/Postal Code _____

Daytime phone number _____
(Area Code)

Return entries with invoice in envelope provided. Each book in this shipment has two entry coupons—and the more coupons you enter, the better your chances of winning!

© 1991 HARLEQUIN ENTERPRISES LTD.   CPS-M1